MW01615747

motored a laugh.

• • • •

The Thunderbird stretched its front tires and they molded into little rubber claws and began to pull the car body forward. It clambered down from the Pyramid and hit the ground at a run and a roar.

Batman floorboarded the Batmobile. He had no other choice but to ram the Thunderbird. There was a noise like a boxer taking a left to the solar plexus.

The Thunderbird rebounded with a scream. It came forward throwing a left jab—a left tire—and popped the Batmobile's windshield and sprayed glass back in on Batman.

The Thunderbird, still on its hind tires, bobbed and weaved, threw another left tire jab, followed it with a right tire cross that stretched the tie rods and the spindle and the tire itself.

Batman stomped the brake, jerked the gearshift into first, stomped the accelerator, tried to ram again. There came a noise from under the hood like someone beating a seal to death with a club and the car clattered forward at a speed that would have embarrassed an amputee turtle.

It spread wide its front tires and grabbed the Batmobile on either side of its doors and pushed, sealing its victim, and Batman inside . . .

•

BATMAN: CAPTURED BY THE ENGINES

BATMAN
CAPTURED BY THE ENGINES

JOE R. LANSDALE

WARNER BOOKS

A Time Warner Company

WARNER BOOKS EDITION

Cover illustration by Dave Dorman

Warner Books, Inc.
666 Fifth Avenue
New York, N.Y. 10103

A Time Warner Company

Printed in the United States of America

First Printing: July, 1991

10 9 8 7 6 5 4 3 2 1

AUTHOR'S ACKNOWLEDGMENTS

It should first be noted that the Manowack Indian tribe is a creation of this writer's imagination, and the creation of that tribe was not due to laziness, but was created to fit into the Batman/Gotham City Alternate Universe. The tribe is not based on any one actual American Indian tribe, but is a combination of many tribes and American Indian mythologies and other mythologies strained through this writer's imagination for the purpose of this story.

Thank-yous are in order for Bob Kane and Bill Finger, who created the Batman, and for Gardner F. Fox, who wrote so many entertaining Batman comics; for Martin H. Greenberg, who first got me involved in writing Batman fiction and fulfilling a childhood ambition; for Robert Simpson and Jim McCann for being so much help; for Bob Wayne, who was my guide through a maze of comics; for Barbara Puechner, friend and agent, who has been with me through thick and thin and knows what it's like to live off moonlight and water; and for all the great pulp writers who knew about action and color.

Special thanks to Ardath Mayhar for the usual support and suggestions, to my daughter Kasey and my son Keith for being as enraptured with Batman mythology as I am, to David Webb for being as crazy as I am, to Roy Orbison and Sam Cooke for poetic background, and more immediately, I would like to dedicate this entertainment to my good friend Scott Cupp for his role in the matter, which included numerous ideas I copped, the *Captured by the Engines* title being most prominent; but most of all, I dedicate this to him for his friendship over the years.

Thanks, Scott. You're the best of pals.

"The new gods are caped crusaders, men of steel. . . ."

". . . we see a society which is militaristic, increasingly mechanized and technologized, which prizes competitiveness and masculine aggression. . . ."

Harold Schechter
author of *The New Gods*

"Every man casts a shadow; not his body only, but his imperfectly mingled spirit."

Henry David Thoreau

BATMAN

CAPTURED BY THE ENGINES

PROLOGUE

Ladies and Gentlemen, Start Your Engines

1

Excerpt from *The Book of the Thunderbird*

In the beginning there was darkness.
Then there were headlights.
On high beam.
And it was good.
Udden, udden.

2

Gotham City: Webb Street and Intersecting Alley, North of the Theater District, July 28th, 11:35 P.M.

Okay, Harders thought, *it could be worse*.

He lay among the garbage and looked across the alley and saw his leg on the far side. The bloody stump, terminating an inch above the knee, rested against a plastic milk bottle that had been knocked free of one of the garbage cans when he had banged into it. The leg had been smacked completely out of his pants, and in fact the pants leg itself had been ripped off as well and thrown God knows where. The shoe he had been wearing had come off the foot and only the sock remained, and his big toe was sticking through it, and that wasn't due to the accident. It had to do with the age of his socks. Pretty embarrassing. He wondered if he had on clean underwear. His mother always warned him to have on clean underwear in case of an accident. Then again, after the whack he took, had they been clean, they might not be now.

Harders felt the urge to crawl across the way and get hold of his amputated leg and find his shoe and slip it on the foot to cover his toe and the worn sock, but that was silly.

Of course it was silly!

He could hardly move, let alone crawl, and he was oozing blood hot and fast and the dark sky above him seemed darker than he'd ever seen it and the alley walls had begun to bend and ripple, as if viewed from beneath great depths of water; the coppery odor of his blood and the rot of the garbage had blended together into a stench that was pounding his nostrils like a fist, and here he was thinking maybe he should find his shoe, cover up his naked toe.

He had to get a grip here, focus on the situation, determine what was truly important. He stayed in Bozo Land much longer, it was all over but the burying.

Harders closed his eyes and took in some deep breaths. It felt as if all his nerves and muscles and veins had been removed and replaced with hot barbed wire and the barbs were doing their best to rip free to the outside.

He opened his eyes. Black dots, like thousands of seed ticks diving down from the heavens, filled his vision.

He closed his eyes again, opened them slowly. The diving seed ticks were gone. His vision, if not his mind, was a little clearer.

He managed to get himself up on an elbow, and gritting his teeth, he dragged himself backwards until his back was against the alley wall. He took a long, hard look at his leg.

And nearly passed out at the sight.

The stump, high above where the knee had been, was squirting blood, and he knew from having worked briefly as an E.M.T. many years ago, he had maybe thirty seconds before he passed out, and if he did pass out, it was *call in the dogs, time and go home*, as his father used to say.

Home. He wished he were there now. Not his apartment here in Gotham City, but his real home. Back in Nacogdoches, Texas, miles and years from here.

He examined his leg again.

Thirty seconds was generous.

Hang in there, he told himself. *It's going to be okay. They may end up calling you stumpy, but it's going to be okay. Better to be called stumpy than to be called dead.*

He unbuckled his belt and tugged it from the pants loops, wound it tight above the wound, and pulled it snug. A last squirt of blood leapt from the nub of his leg and ceased. The seed ticks dive-bombed him again. He closed his eyes and took in deep breaths, and when he opened them the ticks were not completely gone, but they were fewer. There was a coat hanger in the garbage beside him, and now with the flow of blood stanched, he could register enough mentally to see it and take it and wrap the end of the belt around it, then twist the coat hanger tight so that he could keep the blood shut off. That done, he leaned against the wall and tried hard to feel the bricks through his shirt, tried to recognize some sort of feeling other than the pain in his leg, which had gone rapidly from numb, to throbbing, to a slow explosion that began at the wound and went throughout his body like a chain reaction and swelled as if in preparation for the big boom—the kind that could create a new universe.

He tried to remember how this had happened, because it was slipping away, and no matter how this ended up, him dying or surviving, he wanted that much—to remember what had happened.

Then he remembered and wished he hadn't.

He had been with Marilyn. They were on their way to the theater to see a play, a Grand Guignol revival, a thing called "Scream Again," and now here he was, living his own Grand Guignol.

The whole day had been bad, what with him getting up with a crick in his neck and the coffee having brewed bitter and the toast getting burned while he was ironing his shirt, and then the shirt getting burned when he forgot and left the iron resting on the shirt to attend to the toast, and then the argument with Marilyn over her moving in with him immediately instead of next week, and now this.

He'd had some days, but this one took the cake.

Marilyn.

Oh, man, was it ever coming back now. He remembered her flying through the air, her red-blond hair like a burst of sunlight around her head, her blue dress fanned wide like the mouth of a bell.

But why was she flying?

How?

She wasn't any acrobat. They weren't just walking along on their way to the theater and Marilyn suddenly asked that they pause and go into an alley so she could show him a few flips. No, something else.

A car. She had been hit by a car. He remembered it plainly now. That was it. They had been chased into the alley by a car.

They had just crossed the street from Marilyn's apartment, were strolling along, minding their business, arguing some, nothing serious, but arguing now and then about her moving in with him, anticipating the theater a little, worried it might be a dud, this Grand Guignol thing, and talking about how perhaps they should have played it more safely and gone to see "Cats," and Marilyn had said something about her cats, about how they weren't learning to use the litter box, some mundane thing like that, then out in the street a car honked, and they stopped and looked.

It was a black '57 Thunderbird, parked in the middle of the street all by its lonesome, not another sign of traffic in sight. It was as if all the world had disappeared except for this car, and though that alone was weird, there was something about the car that was even weirder. The paint job, for one thing. It was serious black. Harders found himself thinking, *A paint like that, it doesn't come from any store; it comes from the abyss itself—a place where the colors are so dark and deep they give dark a bad name.*

From under the hood chugged a faint puff of steam, like hot breath against frosty air, but it was a warm night, not cold, and then there was the growl of the motor, like a hungry jungle cat, and there was music, crystal clear from the radio or the stereo system inside the car, and though the windows were rolled up, the music, an old Beach Boys tune, "Fun, Fun, Fun," was as clear as if it were playing inside Harder's head. And finally there were the windshields and door glasses, dark all around so no driver was visible, but the glass didn't seem tinted, more like it was filmed over from the inside by greasy smoke.

That damn car made his skin crawl, and Marilyn felt

the same way. He could tell because she reached out and touched his shoulder and her fingers shook as if electrically charged.

"It's okay," he said, and they started walking again. Briskly.

The Thunderbird paced them.

Harders felt an urge to bolt and run, but he didn't let it get the better of him. It was just a car, nothing more.

The Thunderbird gunned its engine, wheeled toward the sidewalk, straight at them. The mouth of a narrow alley was nearby, and Harders grabbed Marilyn's hand, yanked her in that direction and started running.

After that, it all became a blur of Marilyn's long, blond hair trailing behind her and their legs flashing before them (legs, oh, God, did he have to remember legs?), and there was the loud roar of the Thunderbird as it bore down on them, its headlights hot and round and bright at their backs. He could actually feel the heat of the engine at the base of his spine, like some crazed thing breathing on him.

He tossed a look over his shoulder and got a glimpse of the Thunderbird, its windshield a dark, emotionless bug eye with an almost invisible hairline crack on its far left side.

The cacophony of its screaming tires and growling motor mixed together into a sound as wild and savage as the birth of creation, and as a backbeat to it all was the throbbing fanfare of "Fun, Fun, Fun," but Harders and Marilyn weren't having any fun, fun, fun here, not a drop.

Harders jerked his head forward and put everything he had into his running. There was a tug at his hand, and he glanced to see where Marilyn was pulling him, but she wasn't pulling. She had fallen back, lost speed, and had been hit by the Thunderbird and knocked away. What he had felt was her hand torn free of his, and at the moment of that realization he saw their shadows (Marilyn's flipping, his running) on the alley wall, pinned there by the car lights.

Marilyn hit the brick wall, quick and solid with a wet sound, then her shadow disintegrated and the shadow shards bounced back and past him and were sucked into the Thunderbird's headlights. Then Harders was no longer looking. He was yelling and running, the horn of the Thunderbird blaring behind him.

He felt a numbing sensation as he was struck and became airborne. He went high up and fell down dead center of the alley. When he tried to rise, he couldn't—not on both legs, anyway. He still had two then, but one was injured. He got his good knee under him, then *wham*, the bad leg, which dangled behind him like a wet noodle, was hit again, and so was his butt. He was airborne once more, and he knew the car was toying with him, stretching out the fun, making it last. He landed amid a throng of trash cans. The car came again and hit the cans and the cans hit him and he went rolling, garbage falling down on him like an avalanche. When he awoke a few moments later, he was confused and the car was gone, having most likely given him up for dead; and, to understate the situation, he didn't feel good at all.

Now, with his memory of the incident returned, he looked in the direction of Marilyn's demise, saw a smear on the wall and one of her arms sticking up over a mound of garbage. The garbage was twisted and mashed about her. It was obvious the car had run over her repeatedly, as if she were home base and it were playing tag.

He hoped, for her sake, she was dead. And now he determined that if things could be worse, they couldn't be much worse. From where he lay, there was only a hair's difference between sad hope and the worst it could get.

He passed out for a while, and when he awoke there was movement and a shadow.

He looked up, expecting the front end of the Thunderbird, but what he got was a kid about fifteen—a greasy-haired kid in a black T-shirt and blue jeans and sneakers, carrying a leg propped against his shoulder like a baseball player waiting his turn at bat. Harders didn't have to be a mental giant to know whose leg the kid had. He hadn't lost so much blood that he thought people wandered the streets of Gotham with spare legs cocked on their shoulders. The kid smiled down at him. He was missing some front teeth. "You loose something, mister?"

Harders found he couldn't speak. He was too weak. And now the kid looked like two kids standing there, and one kid would go into the other from time to time and there would only be the one kid, then he would separate and make two kids, twin kids with twin legs on their shoulders.

"Looks like a car maybe hit you, huh?" said the two kids before they became one again. "That's bad, man. That could hurt something serious. You know, I like that shoe you got on. Maybe there's one somewhere here to fit this foot." He patted the socked foot of the amputated leg. "I got a foot about this size, I think."

"Nine," Harders said, finding his voice. It came out of him before he knew what he was saying.

"Nine?" the kid said, idly thumbing the big toe poking through the sock. "That's good. I'm an eight and a half myself, but I can wear a nine I put on thick socks, maybe a little newspaper in the toes of the shoes."

"Thick socks," Harders said, and it seemed as if he had spoken some great code word, because suddenly the discussion of shoes and socks seemed very important. You had good shoes, it was important to wear the right socks, even if you had to put newspaper in the toes of your shoes. Had he had on the right socks in the first place, a good, new, thick pair, his toe wouldn't be sticking out like that.

The kid swung the leg and hit Harders with it, right across the bridge of his nose. Harders fell over as if he were a bowling pin, lay on his side with his cheek pressed into the rotted remains of a tomato while the kid hit him with the leg some more.

Harders was stupefied. Could hardly feel the kid's hands on him, going through his pockets, pulling the shoe from his good foot. Being frisked or beaten or hit by a car was all the same to him now. Nothing was of any great importance one way or another.

The coat hanger twisted loose on his leg and he could feel his blood oozing around him in a pool. The pain went away. Fear went away. He felt cozy, as if he were a kid again back in East Texas and it was fall and the window was open and the October night was seeping cool and comfortable into his room, lulling him to sleep.

Then, for a moment, consciousness resurfaced. He knew where he was and what had happened, and before he lost that, before he drifted back down into the pleasantly cool, dark autumn where death awaited him, he thought in a moment of defiance: "I hope the little bastard doesn't find the other shoe."

3

The kid, whose name was Bill Thomas, came out of the alley wearing Harder's shoes—the missing one hadn't been hard to find at all—carrying the leg by the ankle, the bloody end cocked over his shoulder. In his other hand he held Harder's wallet. Marilyn's purse strap was draped over the bend of his elbow.

He leaned the leg against the side of a building, nub down, opened the wallet, and looked inside. Five twenties. Some credit cards.

Two hundred in the purse. Some credit cards.

Man, what a take. And he hadn't had to mug anyone. He'd heard that if you came over to this side of town, you could do better than kicking hell out of some homeless addict in an alley over on the east side, taking his begging change. And he'd heard right. Tonight had been a gift from the gods. He'd heard that old music, the Beach Boys stuff, then he'd heard someone yelling, seen that car come out of the alley.

Weird about that. The car had been in there, certainly, but looking at the alley afterward, he didn't see how. It was pretty wide, but not so wide a car could have turned around in there, let alone made the mess it made of that woman. Just wasn't room for cutting circles like that. Car going in there would most likely be clanging its door handles on the wall a bit.

Still, he'd seen it jet out of there, and not clanging its door handles, shooting into the street like a baby shark being squeezed from the womb, bright and deadly looking beneath the streetlights.

But he wasn't going to worry about it. If the alley was wide enough for only one car and he'd seen five of them come out of there side by side, he didn't give a damn. He wasn't into mysteries. He was into money and buying a little crack now and then. It wasn't like he was an addict or anything. No, sir. He just liked to get high.

Important thing was he'd seen the car come out, and when it was gone, turned down the street fast as lightning, leaving rubber smoke behind it so dark and thick it rose up and temporarily dimmed the streetlights, he walked over to the alley and heard a moan and went in there and saw the mess the car had made, found the tapioca woman and the guy with one leg.

Easy. It had been so easy. He could use the credit cards for groceries and new duds, some of those neat tennis shoes, buy some stuff he could resell later, like TVs and radios. He could buy all that before the cards got canceled.

He put the wallet in his back pocket and snapped the purse shut and let it dangle from his arm while he turned to look at the leg.

Maybe he could sell it to somebody. He knew some

people would like a thing like that. Maybe boil the flesh off and keep the leg bone as a souvenir.

"Excuse me."

Bill jumped at the voice, turned to look at a huge, red-faced beat cop holding a billy club.

"Officer," Bill said.

"I don't suppose that's your purse, now is it, son?"

"It's my sister's. I was taking it to her."

"Taking it to her, you were?"

"Yes, sir."

"And the leg. Does that belong to her too, son?"

"No, sir."

"And I'd be thinking it isn't a leg of your own, seeing as how you have two right on your own body. A spare, perhaps?"

"No, sir. I tell you true, I found that leg."

"Found it, you did? Just lying about?"

"Yes, sir. It was right here leaning against this wall. I saw it and was stopping to look at it." Smiling now. "You don't see that every day."

"No, you don't."

The beat cop looked casually to the mouth of the alley, saw dark skid marks. He looked back at the kid.

"I think maybe you and I should go back in the alley there and have us a look around. You wouldn't mind that, would you, son?"

"Officer, I'd like to help the police, I really would, but my sister's expecting me."

"Son, you have the right to remain silent. You—"

Bill flung the purse into the officer's face and broke for it. The purse didn't do the officer much damage, but it startled him momentarily and the kid got a good start. He went down the sidewalk a block and darted across the street in front of a taxicab that slammed on its brakes long enough for the driver to throw a curse out the window.

The officer, whose name was O'Herity, holding the leg and the purse because he didn't want to leave evidence lying about, came cursing along in front of the cab just as it was about to start up again. The driver yelled after him, "Hey, Officer, that your purse and your mother's leg?"

O'Herity thought, *Fifty thousand comedians out of work, and this guy's got a line. Be glad I'm busy, Mr. Funny Guy.* He pounded on after the kid, followed him down a dark alley.

O'Herity kicked garbage from under his feet and watched the dark shape of the kid reach a chain-link fence, jump up and grab the top of it and pull himself over.

O'Herity cursed more savagely. The last few years he'd put away too many beers and pastramis on rye for that. Ten years ago he could have moved like the kid, but now . . . well, it hurt him to think about it.

Reluctantly, he leaned the leg against the fence, hoping no hungry dogs or cats would come along and steal it, pulled the purse strap high on his shoulder, grabbed the fence and grunted and tugged himself to the top of it, caught a pants leg and ripped it as he more fell than climbed to the other side.

He looked up to see the kid still running. There was another fence at the far end, and O'Herity knew if the kid got over that he was gone, and fast as the kid was moving, that was highly likely.

Still, he had to try. O'Herity hitched the purse up again, started puffing forward, was brought up short.

Out of the darkness that draped into the alley, a big

shadow full of sharp angles and ripples dropped from above and landed lightly in front of the kid and moved from a crouch to a tall, wide, standing shape—the shape of a monstrous bat spreading its wings wide. The kid, going full out, ran right into the bat, and the wings closed around him.

O'Herity stopped and grinned and put his hands on his knees and took in some deep breaths. Nothing to worry about now.

The Batman had him.

[illegible]

sudden fall of [illegible] and [illegible] [illegible] [illegible]
[illegible] [illegible] light. [illegible] of the [illegible] [illegible] [illegible] [illegible] [illegible]
[illegible] [illegible] [illegible] [illegible] [illegible] [illegible]—the [illegible] [illegible]
[illegible] [illegible] [illegible] [illegible] [illegible] [illegible] [illegible] [illegible]
[illegible] [illegible] [illegible] [illegible] [illegible] [illegible] [illegible] [illegible] [illegible]
him.

Hartley [illegible] [illegible] [illegible] put his hands on his knees and took in some deep breaths. [illegible] [illegible] worry about [illegible].

The [illegible] has him.

4

A Back Road Twenty-five Miles Outside of Gotham City in the Great Gotham Valley, Just Before Dawn

It was a joy to run.

Down into a dip in the road it went, the pit-black Thunderbird, happy and vibrant with the joy of destruction, sailing on concrete and wind and four-ply tires, descending into a morning fog thick as the wool on a sheep's back, then up the hill it roared, to the peak, where the warming bulb of the rising sun burned through the haze, thinning it to the consistency of dust motes. On up and out of the valley it charged, until streaks of sunlight swelled and throbbed and the morning bloomed like a red-gold rose.

Clutch and Shift to—

—First Gear

1

Bruce Wayne/Batman's Computer Journal, Morning, July 29th

Alfred, as always, this is for you, my dearest and closest friend.

I find a certain peace in recording what has occurred each night out, and I know, too, that sometimes, face-to-face, I lack the ability to express some of my truer and darker feelings. This way, what I put down is fresher and less likely to be altered by the slipstream of time, and I can record my experiences for possible review at a later date, share them with you—should you have the desire to read my notes—without me actually having to speak my impressions.

Who says the Batman is fearless?

I can face thugs and madmen and guns and knives, the very blazing gates of hell, but when opening the door of my mind and entering into the dark room of my past, I go weak. It is a room I can glance into only in passing. I can never quite encourage myself to step deep into that darkness, lest there is no floor, just the bottomless black.

Pardon the melodrama, Alfred, but I am, after all, in a rather melodramatic business.

So, once again, down here in the bowels of what I in humor refer to as the Batcave, I sit before my computer journal and work the keys and electronically record the events of the night and my impressions, and it has been a long, exhausting night, though little happened specifically to me.

The usual muggers with all the guts of a gnat, springing on an old lady in Crime Alley, not knowing, of course, that I was there and would not allow them to harm her.

I hope their experience with me causes them to retain bad memories and certain reservations about their line of work, though I doubt it.

Bad business out there, Alfred. Crime has always been with us. It was crime that made me who I am. But it has gone from bad and nasty to commonality. That is where my true concern lies: crime's move into the arena of normalcy. Where before it shocked and horrified us, the threat of it now hangs over our lives to such an extent that most have assumed a fatalistic posture, expecting it to eventually overtake us all. And that is certainly possible.

Consider this. Last week. The *Gotham Times*, second page—not even front, mind you—a photograph of kids lined up to board a school bus and they are stepping over a dead body lying in congealed blood, obviously the victim of some crime or fatal accident. The kids in the photograph look as if this is a minor inconvenience, this stepping over a corpse. They might as well be stepping over a mound of garbage.

The body must have been lying there for some time—had to be, for a reporter to be called out to photograph it, and for him to catch those kids just as they boarded the bus. All of this done before a police unit is called, which strikes me as even more cold-blooded. Someone bothers to call in the discovery of a body, and who do they call?

The newspaper.

Maybe because the caller got his name mentioned for finding the body, and that struck him as more important than its removal and the investigation of the crime. How casual can death become?

I digress, as I often do. The thugs were nothing. Didn't even wind me. Thing that got to me, along with this general air of defeat that's washed over our city, was a moment with a drug-crazed kid.

Listen to this: I caught him and found out from the officer who was pursuing him that the kid had been discovered with a purse and a human leg, standing at the mouth of an alley counting stolen money and credit cards.

The officer handcuffed the kid and called a squad car to pick him up, and I went away then, against my better judgment, perhaps, but Jim Gordon has plenty to worry about without me being involved in every odd thing that happens in Gotham. He stays in hot water enough over my nose-poking.

Listen to me rationalize. Truthfully, I am back here with regrets, feeling that I am slipping, avoiding doing what I see as my job, reinforcing my actions by telling myself I am making it easier on Jim, when in fact that is not true.

That kid triggered something in me I preferred not to deal with beyond doing what was absolutely necessary.

That is what took it out of me, gave me this feeling of exhaustion that goes beyond the physical, a feeling nasty and soul-sucking, bottomed out somewhere beyond flesh and blood and bones.

That kid, kids like him, are tossing their lives away, Alfred. Like so much trash in the street. There is nothing I can do but collect it, deposit it where it can be taken care of. At least temporarily, until it slips through the trash compactor we call justice and is recycled back into the inky heart of Gotham City and is finally picked up one last time and permanently disposed of.

Sometimes I feel there is no hope. That what I do is ultimately a colossal waste of time; that I'm nothing more than a pinkie jammed in a hole in the crumbling dike of law and order, and the water-wall of darkness and corruption behind the dike is much too powerful for dike or pinkie; that soon the water will spurt around my finger and the dike will crumble even more, explode into a zillion fragments that will never again be pasted together to hold back the deep, churning waters of fear.

Then again, after a good day's sleep, I may feel differently. I may feel, as I do in rare moments, that I can actually make a difference. The way I sometimes feel when the end of night is near and there has been a light rain and I am crouched atop one of Gotham's great buildings and morning is on the rise, hot pink arteries of sunlight pulsing through the charcoal colored sky, expanding slowly, like the spread of blood poisoning. And, of course, it is just like me to compare even a beautiful sunrise to blood poisoning—but in that fine sweet moment I can crouch in the decaying shadows and feel the cool early morning wind lift my cloak and I can savor its touch on the exposed areas of my face, and there is no stink of garbage from the streets below rising up to fill my nostrils, because the rain has temporarily knocked it down. There are no cries of help or screams of fear to spark through me and set me on fire. It is a time of freshness, renewal. When I can believe I have more than a finger in the crumbling dike of law and order. That I, in fact, have at least two fingers in that hole, and maybe some of the cracks have been glued more soundly than I first realized, and the wall will hold, and gradually a super hot sun will rise above it all and evaporate the sea of crime.

Then those moments will be shattered by moments like the one with that kid. In my mind's eye I see him now—running wild and full of fear down that alley, into my arms—and I am reminded, as I am reminded a million times a day by some little thing or another, of another boy, and that boy is me, and inside will always be me, no matter how old I get.

That boy is also in an alley, only walking home with his parents after a movie, happy, sheltered from true knowledge of the evil that men can do to one another, when out of the darkness comes a man with a gun to introduce him to it.

The man asks for money and the boy's parents respond too slowly. The sweaty hand of the man with the gun jerks, and a bullet leaps out and takes the father down.

Another bullet takes the mother. The robber panics, runs away, leaving the boy beneath a bug-swarmed streetlight, his formerly blissful world crumbling around him like the dike I envision tonight.

Times like these, I think none of my life is real after the time in the alley and the man with the gun. That I am still a little boy, home from having seen *The Mark of Zorro*, and I am dreaming.

In the dream bad things have happened to me. My mother and father are dead and I have grown to become what I am, inspired by that athletic masked man, Zorro. It is a frightening and exhilarating dream, but soon I know I will awake, perhaps with a cry, and my mother will come to me and comfort me, and my father will follow, and he will tell me, "It's okay, son. Just a bad dream. Everything's okay."

And it will be okay.

But I do not awake and find myself young. I awake as I am, in a bed that seems to float in the midst of this great mansion where footsteps echo as empty as the hollow places in my soul.

Other times, I think I took a bullet that night. That I'm lying somewhere in a hospital with liquid-filled tubes attached to my arms, an oxygen mask on my face, aging, imagining this life of mine, a life where a grown man can become one with the shadows and wear the outfit of a bat and strike fear into the hearts and minds of criminals.

Dreaming, drifting down deep into the shadowy subconscious of a coma, just waiting for time to take me away into complete and peaceful darkness where there are no dreams, no emptiness.

Enough of that. No more dark tripping down bad memory lane, lest my life become as pitiful and useless as that of the nihilist of which I am complaining.

Let me end with this: I sense strangeness on the wind, Alfred, and I should know. My life wears strangeness and mystery like a coat—like a cloak, I should say.

If I were writing a blues song I would say bad things are gonna come. Something about tonight. That kid. The hit-and-run in the alley. More than meets the eye going on there.

However, for the moment, the only thing I want to meet my eyes are my eyelids when I close them in sleep.

2

A Little Later

The sun was high but the bedroom was dark. The thick curtains were drawn tight across the wide windows.

A door opened. A thin wedge of light cracked the darkness of the room. A shadowy shape filled the wedge of light, moved, allowed the light again, then the door closed softly and there was darkness.

Alfred Pennyworth, ramrod straight, crisp as ever in his butler uniform, walked quietly and quickly to the bed and looked down on Bruce Wayne's sleeping form. The covers were half thrown off Bruce and he was sleeping naked as always. Alfred could see the man's broad, muscle-twisted back. He could hear Bruce's breathing, slow and steady.

Alfred removed a penlight from his jacket, turned it on, moved the light quickly across Bruce's body and onto the sheet and pillow. There were no bloodstains on either the man or the bedclothes. Breathing was normal. No sign of injury.

He put the penlight away and pulled the covers gently over Bruce's shoulders. He allowed himself a small, quiet sigh. The fearful moment was over.

Many times he'd found Bruce banged and bloody, or sitting up on the edge of the bed, full of anxiety from the events of the night, or suffering from bad midday dreams. But this morning, physically speaking, Bruce, the Batman, had experienced a good night.

Emotionally, maybe not so good. Reading Bruce's computer entries of late, Alfred discerned a deep melancholia descending on the young man, deeper than usual, and he assumed that when he went down to read this morning's entry, it would do nothing to dispel the feeling. Times like this, he thought he could take no more. The fear. The anxiety for Bruce's physical and mental well-being seemed too great a burden to bear.

He knew what he felt must be akin to the way the parent of a teenager feels when the teenager first gets his or her driver's license and stays out too late and the parent sits up waiting—as he always waited, though Bruce was not aware of it—for the child to return home; waiting for the joyful sound of the car engine in the drive or of a door being unlocked, a light on in the bedroom.

Only this was tenfold worse. Worse than when he had served in the British military as a combat medic, because when he bound Bruce's wounds, saw the anger and bitterness in Bruce's handsome face, he could find no distance between himself and the man. This was his boy, his surrogate son, and there was no division between his feelings for Bruce and the feelings he would have had if he had fathered his own son. And Bruce wasn't a teenager. He was an adult who each night went out purposefully into the underbelly of the city, actively seeking out the jaws of the beast.

More often than not, it made Alfred feel helpless, made him long to be anywhere else. Like the theater and the career he had given up. He would fantasize himself in the great roles he had ached to play, like Hamlet and Macbeth—and would have played, had he not retired his ambitions to be nothing more than a butler.

The theater was a fantasy he would have made real, as his mother had made it real. She had so desired it, that to pursue it, she abandoned both he and his father, Jarvis, who remained the butler for Bruce's parents, Martha and Thomas Wayne, for the rest of his life.

But when Jarvis died, and the Waynes were murdered by a street thug, leaving little Bruce behind, too young to fend for himself, Alfred found he was not callous enough to abandon the boy and follow in his mother's footsteps. The beacon of the footlights was not as strong as the need in little Bruce's eyes.

So he had let it all go. But during moments of regret, he would look at Bruce, feel a parental warmth, and know he had made the right decision. That he was more than a butler. And though this did not cure the longing for the stage, it made his decision a livable one.

Alfred said quietly, "I love you, son. Find peace." He left the room, leaving Bruce with his cheerless dreams.

3

And while Bruce Wayne dreams, another writes. . . .

Excerpt from *The Book of the Thunderbird*

According to the mythology of science, the religion of all-knowing truth that changes constantly with new discoveries and the disposition of those recording it, the earth circles the sun.

In fact, our solar system circles the sun, every planet moving beautifully and magnificently about the life-giving orb of Ole Sol, each turning upon its own axis at different speeds, and again around and around this single blazing nucleus, each little wheel pursued by smaller bodies called moons, the moons reacting to the planets in exactly the same way as the planets react to the sun.

Following.

Circling.

Wheels around hubs, or in the broader sense, wheels within wheels, within hubs within hubs.

Round and round we all go, we of humanity not perceiving the whirling movement consciously, but certainly, in spite of the lie of gravity, regarding it on some level; feeling our inner tides wash from side to side and up and down, acknowledging within the primal cells of our brains that each of us is an ever-changing compass needle, heads pointing "north," "east," "south," and "west," all points in-between; experiencing it in a manner akin to lying in a field on our backs with arms outstretched, bodies close to the wheel, throbbing with the truth of movement that our eyes deny. For in such a position, one can literally detect the turning of the earth, the crawling of the sky, can know accordingly that we are but one of the cosmos's contributions to the great wheel.

And if we are not compasses as aforementioned, then we are at least ball bearings packed greaseless within a device that is for us both hub and wheel, spinning forever through the ceaseless dark of space, the light of our sun in our faces from time to time, warming our little hearts and lying to us that everything is bright and okay, but actually existing for quite another purpose, to mock us, and on some level to remind each of us that soon enough our own inner, hot ball of beauty will set in all its golden glory and the truest darkness of all will come upon each of us, and no sun will rise on that.

Ah, the shiny, lying hub of the sun. The hub to which the Sioux attached their flesh with cords and bones and sticks to be pulled and yanked until their skins broke in reverence to it. The hub to which the Manowacks prayed and called to so lovingly, thinking it a spirit, not knowing it was nothing more than a fancy gold hubcap.

Is it any wonder that humankind, knowing instinctively, if not intellectually, that it is part of a greater circle of wheels, should produce the contraption we call the wheel? Then create later, to complement it, combustion engines full of the little fires of the sun?

Is it any wonder that if one group of humankind chose to rule the wheel and learned to love and feed its engines with the desires and hopes of others, to set the engines up as prizes that determine manhood, financial worth, even sex appeal, it would be the white race? Any wonder at all?

Other races have made and followed the wheel, but the white race has built and adored it and the engines that go with it more than any other. And, no doubt, these wheels have driven humankind on to greater and greater technology so that the more "primitive" peoples of the earth can be ground beneath their treads, choked on their exhausts, the ancient chants covered beneath their growls.

Deprived of their own natural magics and powers by the relentless rush of these engines, engines made so that we might circle our own circle at ever faster paces and hurry us along as quickly as possible toward what white man has obviously been driving toward since he deduced his exalted position in the universe—humankind's self-destruction. Is it any wonder the magics of birds and animals have become nothing more than flesh to die out and rot and turn to fossil fuel, later to be brought up by a drill bit and a wildcat well?

No wheel, that was the Indian's downfall. No wheel to

which to tie his magic. No wheel to which to tie his own engine and ride away from the white man, or better yet, over white man, and cease that race's relentless push toward annihilation.

No wheel for the injun because the wheel hates the earth. No engine for the injun because the engine hates the earth. The wheel crushes, the combustion engine stinks the air.

The Indian is closer to the old nature. But nature has changed. The old girl has died out and a new natural order has taken the throne. Smokestacks, racing engines, and clanging machinery.

The wheel.

The damn wheel. . . . Round and round it goes . . . and goes and goes and goes, and hooked to an engine, it goes faster and faster . . . and faster.

Ancestors, help me. I love it so.

4

Town of Cold Shepherd, Fifty-eight Miles Outside of Gotham City, July 29th, 8:08 P.M.

Cold Shepherd, population five thousand, was characterized by two things: (1) a certain desolation, like an oasis in the wastelands of the Sahara, (2) a solitude broken only occasionally, and that generally on Saturday nights by the usual offenders.

This simplicity of existence, this now-and-then-shattered tranquility, was what had attracted Pale Boy to the job of sheriff. That, and the fact he had achieved a certain modicum of respect, a commodity sorely lacking on the reservation where he was born and raised to adulthood.

In spite of his pale skin—the source of his spoken name, if not his real name—it was no secret to Cold Shepherd that he was a Manowack Indian, and that being known, there was occasional anti-Indian sentiment. But his light complexion did benefit him in the white community, as did his record as an M.P., a record so good it overshadowed the fact that he had been discharged from the military due to a head injury in a bar scuffle arrest with a drunk not quite the size of Pikes Peak. It had been a righteous arrest, but the military saw it as an injury in the line of duty and put him out on the street with an honorable discharge and a series of temporary checks that roosted in his mailbox come the end of every month.

In many ways, he considered his cracked head a benefit. He had gotten out of the military without losing the prestige acquired there, yet he was not disabled. Except for occasional headaches (tonight he had one), admittedly more intense in the last six months, he felt he had gained more than he had lost by the incident.

The fact that the job of sheriff in Cold Shepherd didn't pay him a lot certainly didn't hurt the feelings of the white citizens, and this fact helped Pale Boy to keep it. Except for a couple of well-known incompetents, no one wanted Pale Boy's low-paying job. Not yet, anyway, and the more it could be forgotten that he was Indian, the better the likelihood he could keep his position.

Pale Boy had no qualms about his white metamorphosis. In fact, he often dreamed of it. In these dreams he was a giant Kafkaesque cockroach wrapped in a bright Manowack blanket with pounds of turquoise jewelry—never mind the fact that the Manowack had never dealt with turquoise; it was one of those modern symbols of Indianhood that manifested itself in his dreams—hanging from his many limbs, and suddenly he would flex and the blanket would rip, the jewelry would fly from him with a clatter, and his roach crust would crack open and he would crawl forth a fresh, pinkish white man craving a martini and the business section of the *Gotham Times* or the *Wall Street Journal*.

His brother, Abner, could cling to the reservation and its boxed-in existence, but he preferred being free of tribal shackles. The Manowack were on a road to extinction as certain and final as that traveled by the dinosaur and the five-cent candy bar.

The earth spins. Times change.

Stepping off the sidewalk into the street, Pale Boy noted that, as usual, there was not a car in sight. Not even a pedestrian. Just after eight o'clock Saturday night, and everyone had gotten where they were going. What action there was would be some teenage excitement at the Big Burger in the form of jukebox music, loud talk, and some heavy necking out back in the parking lot.

About eleven or twelve, Roy Fish and Jimmy Alexander would get in their weekly Saturday night slugfest and end up dotting each other's eyes. The brawl, as always, would conclude with the two of them chipping in to pay for damages to the Shepherd House Bar and swearing on their mothers' graves never to toss knuckles at one another again.

There might also be some action over at the Simmons' place if they decided to have another of their marital squabbles. Then Pale Boy would have to go over there or send his deputy, Herkemer, to put an end to it.

If Bobbie Simmons had taken up her trusty skillet again, he'd probably have to call a doctor to count the knots on Clyde's head. Then, too, there would be the ice pack for Bobbie's eyes, which often matched those of the brawling Fish and Alexander to such a degree that Pale Boy thought of suggesting they form their own singing group and call themselves the Rocking Raccoons—though they would probably be happier as tag team wrestlers.

And of course there would be the town drunk, Evan Hill. He spent about three nights a week in jail, and he was damn proud of it. Saturday night was his biggest night to howl, and he would most certainly have to be arrested.

But for the most part, life was good. Pale Boy had no real hassles. He had a job he liked. Respect. Even a woman he cared about. And best of all, he had left the reservation far behind. So far behind that on a clear day he hated to look in its direction.

He had not seen his brother in years—not that his brother would care to see him—and he felt that Abner was most likely following in the hated footsteps of their father. There was really nothing else for him to do but to inherit the car lot and sell wrecks and smash them up for scrap. The demand for a medicine man, a master of the old ways, was not great in these times. For that matter, when they were boys the demand was not considerable, as their grandfather, Jerome Horse Handler, had attested.

The Manowacks were changing even then, and if not happily, rapidly, if only in surface ways. He remembered how the shacks on the reservation had added electricity as soon as it became available, stuck up TV antennas and parked aged, tall-finned Cadillacs in their front yards. Yards often full of rusted refrigerators and washing machines that had been bought used and worn out completely by being plugged in and kept on outdoor porches as if they were ornate lawn furniture. The elements ate them like snacks, and their rusted crumbs were tossed in the yards and replaced by more used appliances, at what was for the Indians great expense. But the desire to keep up with the

Joneses had spread from the white communities like a disease and infested even the Manowacks. They had moved up from being despised Indians to Indians who lived like poor white trash, and they saw it as good. It was pathetic. So pathetic, Pale Boy had to get away.

Considering how Abner hated their father, and their father's desires to be part of the white world, if he had pursued their father's career, nothing could be more ironic, unless it was the fact that at heart, Abner loved cars and loved rock 'n' roll as much as he professed to hate all things white; loved them but couldn't reconcile them with the old magics and the old ways. Yet Pale Boy was certain Abner had been unable to take to the mountains and live with the wind and the stars and the soil. Those ways were lost forever.

But Pale Boy felt that was no longer his concern. He was gone from there and gone for good.

After a long moment of looking at the partial moon rise above the street, he shook off his memories of the reservation and his brother, adjusted his Stetson, crossed the street, and started making his rounds, trying to will the ache in his head away.

5

8:15–8:21 P.M

Evan Hill, drunker than the proverbial skunk, clinging to a lamppost as if he were making love to it, saw the first bloody disaster about three minutes after Pale Boy vacated the sidewalk and disappeared across and down the street.

Evan had missed the sheriff by a minute or so and he was disappointed. He was ready for his bed and board now. He knew Pale Boy's schedule perfectly, and yet, drunk as he was, he could not make himself arrive on time at a rendezvous point. He had missed the sheriff twice already, and now three times.

The idea was to rest a bit, get a second wind, and catch up with his bed and meal ticket at the Shepherd House Bar. He figured he could make a fool out of himself there as easy as anywhere else, and Pale Boy would arrest him.

A minute passed.

Evan was holding the pole with one hand now, about

to let go and launch himself a-sail across the street, when he heard the music. He recognized the tune. "Our Car Club," by the Beach Boys, and by golly, he loved it. He loved all their music, but especially the car songs. The sound of it made him wish he still had a driver's license. A car, for that matter. Last time he'd seen his old Buick was a long time back and from a prone position after he had drunkenly piled into a tree and been thrown free of it. The Buick hadn't looked too good.

Looking down the street in search of the music's source, he saw nothing. The spot where the sound came from was only shadows—shadows hanging thick as giant batwings between the low-slung buildings at the deep end of the street.

At that moment Evan saw Martha Lynn Peel, the town librarian, come out of the library, long since closed for the day, about a block up with a book under her arm.

Martha's book was a romance, and she clutched it tightly. She looked down the street and saw Evan grasping the lamppost. She thought: *Evan has his post and his bottle and I have my book and my daydreams, and we have nothing else. We are quite a pair of losers.*

It was a thought that came to her abruptly, and not one she ever consciously admitted harboring—that she was no less a loser than the town drunk. She had her books, but she had no life outside of them. She read of men and women in love, of romance, of exotic places, but she had no romance of her own and the most exotic place she had ever seen had been photographs of Borneo in a geography book.

Her life was a walk to work and the dust from books, a dive into a romance novel late at night—a dive deep and far away from the drab, silent walls of her little duplex with its plastic-covered furniture, as if she needed covers for furniture that was so rarely sat on.

Once, a man had been sent by the landlord to fix her water heater, and she had invited him in and fixed him coffee and sat beside him and shown him a travel magazine and had talked foolishly about a resort in Greece she had read about. He had been polite, but she could tell he wanted to be anywhere else but with her; but she couldn't stop talking, flipping the pages and showing him the pictures, and pretty soon she was dripping tears on the magazine, and out of the clear blue, as if struck by a dark, nostalgic thunderbolt, she told him about when she was a girl, about how her father had died of a stroke when she was only five and how her mother had believed that child rearing was a scientific experiment where if you must—must—kiss your child good night, you should do it lightly and briefly on the cheek. Hugs were not permitted.

When the workman left she sat on the couch and curled up in a fetal position and cried so violently her rib cage ached, and now when she saw the workman from time to time on the street, he always looked away or up, as if spotting a rare bird on the wing, some remarkable sight he could not pull his eye from until he had passed her by.

Her thoughts were diluted by the music, and she turned and looked for its source but couldn't locate it. It seemed to be coming from all directions, and from no direction at all, sometimes distant, as if heard through stretched-wire-and-tin-can phones, sometimes close, as if its origin was in her head: a rocking little melody bouncing against the chattel of her memories.

She decided the music must be drifting from some building nearby, echoing down the street. She glanced at Evan again and he smiled at her. After her feelings of loneliness, she felt she should be more sympathetic to poor Evan, but she found she could not. Along with her stiff upbringing she had also been taught the caste system, one where she and her family were placed morally and emotionally head and shoulders above most, and the training died hard. She looked away, checked in the other direction. A cool wind came up and bunched her dress around her legs, carried a candy wrapper down the street. The wind passed on as quickly as it had come up, and Martha stepped off the curb.

And that's when the lights came on.

The lights swelled out of the dark at the far end of the street. Two of them. Spaced side by side, maybe six feet apart. They were at first like the beams of distant lighthouses cutting through a thick-as-pea-soup fog; then they became brighter, like enormous suns burning against the blackness of space.

The music was coming from the direction of the lights. Martha knew that now. It was as if her ears had suddenly sharpened. And the lights were headlights. She couldn't see the car behind them, but instinctively she knew what they were, though they were brighter than any headlights she had ever seen, high beam or otherwise. If she had any doubts about the origin of the lights, they were dispelled when she heard the hum of the motor, soft and hypnotic.

The lights leapt and the purr of the engine became a growl, and Martha, two steps off the curb, knew she was in trouble. The curb behind her seemed far away, and the curb before her somewhere over the rainbow.

The lights swelled and threw Martha's shadow down the street, across the lamppost where Evan dangled like a plastic monkey on a soft-drink straw.

Martha tried to turn and scramble back to the curb, but suddenly she was spinning, legs splayed, like a ballerina making a difficult leap and whirl.

She came down hard on the windshield, her left eye pressed against the glass. She could dimly see inside the car, and what she saw brought a scream to her throat. She attempted to let it out, but it wouldn't come. She didn't have the wind for it; it lodged inside her like a frightened critter in a burrow.

Finally she squeaked and went silent.

A dark swath of blood filmed her left eye. The car reversed and she slid off of it. It came forward again, fast, hot, and furious, minus great gaps in time and space, and once more she was hit. She went low, skimming over the street this time, and though the events were accelerated, her brain slowed them to a crawl.

She hit the street, fish-flopped and rolled, then lay stunned and bleeding. She could hear Evan screaming in terror in the background, then she heard the engine, loud and terrible, then the headlights sprang toward her again.

In the quick instant before it was all over, she saw tire treads full of dirt and pebbles and a bottle cap, then her mouth was full of rubber and the taste was surprisingly salty; her head felt as if it were a balloon in the hands of a cruel child pressing it from all sides. Then she thought no more as skull shrapnel, brains, flesh and blood, and escaping dreams mushroomed into a wet bomb that splattered in all directions, and the great shadow that was hers, lying beside her on the street like something spilled, shot toward the headlight beams and fractured, and the headlights pulled in the fractured shadow and darkness whirled once around them like fouled water swirling in a gutter. Then there was no shadow at all, just the bright hot lights and the growl of the engine and the sour-sweet smell of exhaust.

Evan had a scream in his throat, and unlike Martha's, it found release, and when it did, it came out long and loud and would not cease. A choirboy would have coveted its high range.

A black Thunderbird had hit Martha and killed her, and was spinning bloody doughnuts on what was left of her body.

The Thunderbird stopped abruptly, as if it had exhausted all joy, its nose pointed slightly askew of the street, its left headlight dead-solid perfect on the pole to which Evan, now sober as a Baptist preacher, clung.

Evan knew what was coming, and he started up the pole like a frenzied squirrel. He was only a few feet up when the Thunderbird was there. It hit the pole and the pole whipped back, and Evan went back with it and let go. He was catapulted against a building and into the indention of a recessed but closed doorway.

He sat up, back against the door, legs jutting straight onto the sidewalk beneath the front of the car, its motor throbbing pleasantly, a headlight on either side of him, shiny grillwork in his face, close enough to kiss. He was insanely reminded of a girl he had once loved who wore braces.

With a screech, the car jetted backwards, hit the pole

again, knocked it flat, twisted suddenly, as if made of rubber, acquired the street.

A heartbeat and the car came again, angling this time so that it gained the sidewalk, right tires in the street, left on the sidewalk. Its door handles and hubcaps scraped the building wall, tossed up brick dust.

The left tires went over Evan's legs, and the car wheeled back into the street, spinning so that it was facing him again. It had happened so fast he hadn't had time to recoil his legs or understand what was happening. He was beyond pain.

He looked down to see that from knee to shin his legs were flat. His untouched ankles and feet in shoes looked bloated and ridiculous, like heavy weights at the ends of a drooping wax sculpture.

He lifted his head, heavy as a bowling ball now, just in time to see the Thunderbird's bumper coming for him, smashing the bricks on either side of him, driving him backwards into the doorway, the wood of the door cracking almost as loud as the bones in his chest.

With a shriek of tires, the Thunderbird backed, wheeled, zoomed down the street, returned to darkness, radio blaring the Stray Cats' "Hot Rod Gang."

An instant later the drifting notes of the song could be heard on the outskirts of Cold Shepherd, followed by the sound of happy horn honking—a bully bellowing triumph.

Then the horn went silent and there was only the faint noise of Evan's blood dripping off the shattered doorway onto the sidewalk.

6

8:30 P.M.

Jack was mostly called the Indian Kid, which was only half right, because he was only half Indian. He didn't know the white half that had helped create him; the scoundrel had split the scene before he was born, and his mother—a Manowack—had gone belly-up from an alcohol-riddled liver before Jack had the chance to learn the difference between breast milk and one-hundred-proof whiskey. His mother had thought a white man could get her off the reservation and out of that life of tin shacks and sagged-at-the-axle travel trailers.

But that hadn't been the case. The white man had helped make Jack, but after that he found pressing matters elsewhere. Jack ended up being raised by his uncles, staying with one, then another, but none of them could give him the time and the attention he needed. They were elderly, with bitterness to nurse and livers of their own to poison. He mostly raised himself.

Now, just turning eighteen, he had become complacent, if not comfortable, with the fact that he had seen about as good as he had to look forward to; he could only hope things didn't get worse.

He was walking down Main Street, thinking all this, hands in pockets, head slightly hung, defying any traffic to come along and make him move, when he thought he saw a dead deer in the road—a deer that had been run smack-dab over in the middle of the street.

He raised his head for a better look. The deer was wearing clothes and the clothes were women's clothes, and somehow that struck him as funny—a dead deer in a woman's clothes.

But it wasn't funny long, because the deer had fingers —human fingers. There was an arm sticking out of one of the sleeves, and the hand was open, palm up, flattened like a sausage patty, and there were fingers jutting out of the patty and they had pink-painted nails.

Jack stumbled to the side of the street, no longer willing to defy traffic, no longer even wanting to pretend that was his aim.

It wasn't any better on the sidewalk. Over there, blended in with smashed bricks and a shattered wooden door, was another mess.

Jack broke into a run for the sheriff's office.

8:40 P.M.

Jack found Deputy Herkemer and Herkemer called the chief of the volunteer fire department, who also operated

Cold Shepherd's one-car ambulance service, and told him to hustle up some men and get on over to Main. He left Jack at the office nursing a cold drink and a bag of pork rinds, drove over to the Shepherd House, but found Pale Boy had not arrived on schedule.

This upset Herkemer to no end. He feared he would have to go over to the site by himself, and to date, the worst highway accident he'd seen was a coyote that had wandered out of the woods and into the path of a semi highballing toward Gotham.

If he had to see bad business, human slaughter, he wanted someone with him, someone who had to be more responsible than he. Someone like Pale Boy.

But Pale Boy wasn't there, and just when Herkemer felt fate had him elected, and his stomach had begun to boil in response to the inevitable, the sheriff walked into the bar. Herkemer's stomach ceased to roll, went to a slow simmer. He collected Pale Boy and gave him the scoop while he wheeled them on over to Main.

9:05 P.M.

When Pale Boy got out of the car, he saw the ambulance parked at the curb, the one old fire engine the town owned parked across one end of the street. A few pale-faced onlookers had gathered. The volunteer fire department—only three had shown up—had obviously seen nothing quite so grim before. They were sitting on the curb near the ambulance taking shallow breaths. An empty stretcher lay on the sidewalk behind them. They were looking away from the bodies, and when Pale Boy saw the bodies, he felt the same way.

The world slowed down and it seemed as if his senses heightened; the expanse of his vision was more complete and colors were brighter and richer and the sound of the wind was loud and his nostrils flared with the stench of death.

Catherine Meadows was there, too, slightly pudgy, wearing brown coveralls, her long gray hair tied back at the neck, her face looking ten years younger than her fifty-three years. She was one of four doctors in town, and generally considered to be the best. She served in a limited capacity as Cold Shepherd's coroner. When Pale Boy applied for the job of Sheriff in Cold Shepherd, she had been the one to give him his physical and mental examination. She had become something of a friend.

Pale Boy reasoned she had heard about the hit-and-run—for it was rather obvious to him that's what he was looking at—on her scanner. Formerly of Gotham City, she had worked in hospitals both on the medical side and the psychiatric side (she had notable credentials for both), as well as for the coroner's office. She had seen enough grimness for multiple lifetimes. Gang fights where the action had been so hot and brutal, the remains of the victims had looked like nothing less than the end results of a red paint explosion. Mistreated children. Battered wives and gut-shot thugs, throat-slit pedestrians, gangland murders performed with Louisville Sluggers and plumbing pipe.

Pale Boy assumed there was more to her leaving Gotham than she was willing to admit, but she once told him that seeing all she had seen was why she left the city when she turned fifty. She wanted to get away from the really bad stuff, go on over to little Cold Shepherd and grow a garden, treat a few coughs, tell some folks to turn their heads and cough, and if she had to, look at a dead body once in a while.

Now here she was, looking at two dead bodies as bad as anything she might have seen in Gotham.

Pale Boy left Herkemer standing nervously by the car, walked over to Catherine, slowly.

The pacing didn't help. A cool sweat collected on his forehead. He focused his attention on Catherine. Her face showed no sign she was bothered. She seemed professional and very collected. She was kneeling by the body in the street, writing rapidly in shorthand in a little notebook.

"Catherine," Pale Boy said.

She looked at him and bobbed her chin.

"No accident," he said.

Catherine turned back to look at the body. "This was done for fun."

Pale Boy felt the old crease along his scalp throb, as if someone were in there trying to chisel his way out. "Any idea who it is?"

Catherine pulled a pair of plastic gloves from her back pocket, slipped them on, and poked at the open, blood-splattered romance novel lying amid the mess; it looked like some sort of exotic bird shot down for sport. She removed from beneath it a wet purse. She snapped it open, reached inside, took out a wallet, flipped it open to the driver's license photograph—Martha Lynn Peel's photograph. She held the wallet in Pale Boy's direction. He didn't take it. He said, "Okay."

Catherine closed the wallet, returned it to the purse, snapped it shut, laid it down carefully.

Pale Boy glanced at the body on the sidewalk wedged

against a broken door. It was a wreck, but not as wrecked as the one at his feet. He saw immediately it was his frequent tenant, Evan Hill.

"And Evan?" Pale Boy asked.

"Our erstwhile rescue team says he's dead," Catherine said.

He reached into his shirt pocket, took out the tin of aspirins he had started carrying, opened it, chewed three of them slowly, allowed their bitter tang to kill the coppery taste of blood on the tip of his tongue.

Catherine looked up, watched him return the tin to his pocket, said, "Bad?"

Pale Boy shook his head. "As compared to this, not so bad."

"I guess not. Better have these bodies put on ice. There'll be autopsies. We're going to need some out-of-town pros, and we need the bodies in good shape. Or rather, no worse shape than they're in."

"All right," Pale Boy said.

Catherine stood, went over to Evan's body on the sidewalk.

Pale Boy looked down at Martha's body, took a deep breath, and called to the volunteers, "Load this one first. When they're both loaded, take them over to the locker plant. Call ahead and tell Kravin to open up for you."

One of the men on the curb said, "Mr. Kravin may not like that, us putting them in there."

"I don't care what he likes," Pale Boy said. "Tell him meat's meat. I'm not asking him to process or eat it, just keep it awhile."

The three men looked at one another. The one who had spoken before stood up and stared at Pale Boy, as if to let it register that he could see the sheriff was not a white man, but a Manowack. He said, "Remember, you made us do it."

"I'll write it down," Pale Boy said.

The other two stood, but didn't move in the direction of the body.

"Well," Pale Boy said.

The two who had gotten up last reluctantly took hold of the stretcher, and the three of them went over to Martha's body, studied it, appearing no less ill than they had appeared while seated on the curb.

"What's to pick up?" one of them said. "What's needed here is a hose."

"Do what you can," Pale Boy said.

That's when Catherine said, "Forget the dead one. Haul ass on over here. This one's alive."

7

10:15 P.M.

Pale Boy and Herkemer went to the office and made out reports, then drove over to the hospital and went upstairs to look in on Evan. He was sedated and bandaged, looked like an amputee version of King Tut lying in bed. They stood over him and watched, as if some great revelation would be revealed. Now and then Evan opened his eyes and rolled them around and saw nothing, pursed his lips and fluttered them, made little motor sounds and a noise like a car horn honking, said "Thunderbird," then he'd go silent for a while.

Dr. Catherine Meadows came in and stood by them and looked at Evan. She was out of the coveralls and was dressed in her usual sloppy attire: tennis shoes, old paint-stained dungarees, and a loose-fitting Hawaiian shirt with a red background and a spattering of blue and green palm trees on it.

"When will he be able to talk about what happened?" Pale Boy asked Catherine.

Catherine shook her head. "Can't say. Shock's got him for a while. He's lost a lot of blood. Drugs I gave him will have him out of it too. We may transfer him to Gotham, if his signs don't get any better. All in all, I'd say it'll be a while before we can let him ooze back into reality, and when we do, bet he's gonna want to go back to dreamland." She paused. "And maybe not. What happened to him tonight might be worse inside his head. He can keep replaying it. Least, out here in the conscious world, it's over."

"Why Martha and Evan?" Herkemer said.

"That's your job," Catherine said. "I just patch 'em up."

They retired to Catherine's hospital office and took seats. She locked the door, opened her desk drawer, took out a bottle of whiskey and three paper cups.

"No, thanks," Pale Boy said. "Never touch the stuff."

Herkemer looked at Pale Boy. "Am I on duty?"

"Not right now."

"Then fill it to the brim," Herkemer said. Catherine did, and Herkemer sipped and frowned and smiled afterwards. "Cuts the hair."

"Yeah," Catherine said. "And grows it places you need it most." Catherine gulped her drink three times, poured another, stopped, and removed a bag of tobacco from her shirt pocket and some rolling papers. She rolled a cigarette precisely and swiftly and put it in her mouth but didn't light it. "I don't smoke 'em, I roll 'em and lip 'em. Last step before quitting. Doctor like me, lungs I've seen on X rays, I got to shake the habit."

"I tell myself that too," Herkemer said. "But . . ." He got out a cigarette and poked it in his mouth and lit it and sucked in deep. "I'm still putting fire to them."

"You know," Catherine said, rolling her cigarette to the other side of her mouth, "you boys ought to think about giving the city council some hell. Get them to push for a fire department, an official one with an ambulance branch, operated by real grown-ups with brains and everything. Those volunteer bozos are about as competent as knit prophylactics. They're just volunteers so they can have meetings now and then and get drunk while they wear red fire hats and watch a stag film, see some naked bimbo tie her legs in a knot. Real fire happened, they wouldn't think to piss on it, let alone roll out a hose."

Pale Boy laughed. "We'll get a fire department when something belongs to one of the council members burns down."

"Now there's an idea," said Catherine, seeming to consider it.

"Don't do it when I'm looking," Pale Boy said. He pulled the tin of aspirins from his pocket, opened it, and chewed three of them.

"Hasn't been that long since you took some of those," Catherine said. "You're chewing them too close together, you know?"

"I tell him the same thing all the time," Herkemer said. "Last few months, he's been popping those things like candy."

"Yeah," Pale Boy said, "but my headache hasn't read about the prescribed dosage. It doesn't seem to care what's proper."

"That old wound the problem?" Catherine asked.

"Could be. Anything you can tell us about the bodies might help determine who did this?"

"Nope. But maybe we'll learn something tomorrow after the autopsy. I've called in some bigwigs in Gotham who specialize in this kind of thing, and I'm no slouch myself, so we might find a clue."

"I always figured clues were for mystery novels," Herkemer said.

"They are, most of the time. But little things can add up. One time when I worked for the coroner's office in Gotham, we proved a hit-and-run because the murderer hit his victim and didn't kill him, and when the victim tried to rise, the killer went at him again. Hit him in the chest with the front of the car. License number got imprinted in the victim's flesh in big welts. We held a mirror up to him and got the numbers straight, pulled the guy in who owned the car, and he confessed. He'd killed him over a football bet, something like that."

Catherine plucked the cigarette from her lips and tossed it in the trash can beside her desk. "I'm doing better. I don't keep it in my mouth so long. . . . Pale Boy, that headache keeps up, you ought to come in and let me take a look at you."

"I'll keep that in mind."

Catherine lifted her cup and disposed of her whiskey with a single toss. She made a face, swung her tongue across her lips to swath up survivors, wadded up the paper cup and tossed it in the trash can, and said, "Well, boys, what say let's go home and have bad dreams?"

8

10:59 P.M.

The night was cool and crisp for July, almost fallish, the partial moon as gold as a banker's watch. Pale Boy and Herkemer stood by the car and looked up at the moon and then out at the quiet town. Herkemer sighed and opened the car door. Before he could slide behind the wheel, Pale Boy said, "I'll walk. Maybe some fresh air will help clear up this headache."

Herkemer nodded. "All right. Me, I'm not walking anywhere, not after tonight."

"Yeah, well, I'm sort of a believer in odds. Two in one night ought to be enough to please fate."

"I got no faith in fate," Herkemer said. "See you in the morning."

"Yeah."

Herkemer drove away and Pale Boy began to walk. When he came to Main Street, he glanced at the spots where Evan and Martha had been found, saw the fire department had hosed the streets clean of blood. The rubber burns on the concrete were still visible, however, and the concrete on the sidewalk where the lamppost had stood was broken open and pouched up like a savage skin eruption.

Pale Boy thought of Martha's body down at the locker plant, wrapped in plastic and arctic cold, sides of beef and pork hanging around her like decorations. He tried to summon up her image before destruction, and managed, but it was a dim recollection, and somehow more painful than seemed reasonable for a person he hardly knew.

She had been a quiet, almost mousy woman, and he couldn't remember if he had ever spoken to her, except perhaps in casual greeting. He remembered best the way she had looked there in the street, far more brutalized than any meat at the locker plant.

He thought of Evan, his regular guest at the jail. A drunk, but not a bad old guy; not too unlike a lot of Pale Boy's Indian relatives who had found their lives intolerable except for when the whiskey took them away to a more pleasant place.

When he crossed the street, he was more careful than usual, and halfway across he was assailed by a feeling of dread. But no cars leapt out of the dark and no motors hummed in the distance. By the time he reached the sidewalk on the other side, his forehead was beaded with sweat. He moved between two dark buildings, down a darker alley, and then the moonlight overhead went away and a shadow glided across his path and turned the blackness blacker. Pale Boy looked up and saw the source of the shadow drifting over the top of one of the buildings, and even at a glance, as it floated out of sight and the moonlight came back, he knew it was an owl. One of the ancient Manowack totem spirits.

And as the shadow passed from view, he found himself dreaming awake—a dream of a young boy hanging by what appeared to be a rope, hanging in darkness, the body gone purple like an overripe grape about to fall off the vine.

The dream faded as instantly as it had come, leaving his head with a greater ache. He tried to recall something that might have triggered the waking dream, but could not. Unless it was the owl, and he couldn't calculate how the owl could have triggered anything other than memories of the old ways, superstitions like the Owl God, the ugliness of the reservation. And those were not memories he purposely dealt with.

Still, there was something immediate about what his mind's eye had revealed, but the immediacy faded. The more he tried to recall the vision, put some meaning behind it, the more his head hurt, so he gave it up, walked on, trying to concentrate on something more pleasant and understandable.

Home and Angie, his white woman.

White woman.

That's what he thought as he walked, and it embarrassed him. It was a primitive and childish thought, and he knew it, but there seemed absolutely nothing he could do about it. It would surface in his subconscious from time to time like a shark (a great white?) rising for floating chum, and then he would knock it back, as if he were a fisherman batting it with a heavy boat paddle, but as soon as he relaxed his guard, up it would come again, mouth wide open and hungry.

White woman.

Angie had much to recommend her as a person, but he knew in his heart it always came down to that. There was no denying it. It was the major thing that had attracted him to her. She was blond, fair-skinned, blue-eyed, and white. White women had always been his failing, and once, one had been Abner's.

A blond-eyed beauty of an anthropologist out from Gotham, come to study the Manowack—maybe to figure out if they got good television reception or something—had trapped Abner's heart as expertly as Abner could trap rabbits. But like a hunter who takes one of his catches as a pet and eventually tires of it and lets it go, she let Abner go. It made him hate the whites more.

Pale Boy, on the other hand, felt quite differently on the matter, and having abandoned the Manowacks, found it only fitting to have himself a white woman. It was another step away from the reservation, into white society and respect.

"Uncle Tomahawk"—that's what Abner would call him. And he would not be wrong. Not at all. But in Pale Boy's mind, it beat being a ragged-ass Indian.

11:16 P.M.

Angie answered the door wearing jeans and a T-shirt spattered with red paint. The red paint sent Pale Boy's mind whirling back to Main Street, where the red he was looking at had not been paint. He put that out of his mind by studying Angie, a sure cure for most of what ailed him. Her curly blond hair was tied back from her attractive, pink-cheeked face with a black ribbon and she was barefoot. Her feet had red paint sprinkled on them. She held the paintbrush cocked in her right hand as if she planned to slap Pale Boy with it. She wasn't smiling, but there was humor on her face. "About time you showed up, Tonto."

Pale Boy didn't like the Indian jokes at all, didn't like to be reminded constantly of his Indian heritage, but he never let on, and in order to convince himself it didn't matter, he always played back. "You're still up?"

"Very observant."

"And you're on the warpath?" There, he'd done it. He'd made an Indian joke.

"Yep."

"Well, sweetheart, way it works is you paint your face, not your feet. I've seen cowboy and Indian movies, and that's the way the Indians do it when they're on the warpath. They paint their faces."

"I'm sure I have paint on both, thank you." She leaned forward and kissed him lightly on the lips. "Get your sorry self inside."

He stepped inside and tossed his Stetson on the couch. "This warpath you're on got anything to do with me?"

She led the way to the kitchen. "Some," she said. "You have lousy hours. You've been spending more and more time away from home lately."

"Work," he said.

"Yeah, and what's her name?"

He thought, *Tonight her name is Martha*, but said, "Lady Fate."

"A tip, Tonto. You got to have good lies ready, you want to please me. And that one, it wasn't so good."

"Are you really hacked? That why you've got me standing in the doorway?"

She grinned and stepped aside. "Yeah, I'm hacked, but the real reason is this kitchen."

Stepping into the kitchen, Pale Boy saw immediately what she meant. She had been livening up the counters and cabinets with red and blue paint, a plan that struck him poorly. Early mornings he didn't like the idea of being assaulted by primary colors. He liked it mild and calm and tan or beige, but then again, Angie saw this as stodgy. But, color disagreements or not, the fact remained: Angie was a lousy painter—at least in the normal sense of the word—and there was the wry rub. She was, by profession, an artist, and a brilliant one. Her sculptures and paintings hung in museums and galleries throughout the United States. She often had one-woman shows in Gotham. On canvas her hand was sure and inspired. Sadness and passion, love and loneliness came out of her fingertips then, went right into the paint and coiled there like a living thing. But any sort of domestic chore escaped her. It was as if her hands turned to salad tongs then. She couldn't paint a straight line, couldn't keep the paint even, her mind wandered.

"You need to paint one direction," he told her. "Not every which way."

"There's no imagination in this sort of thing," she said.

"You need to keep your paint even. And you need more newspaper down. You're getting it on the floor."

She handed Pale Boy the brush. "There you are," she said.

"Hey, you know, this really looks great. I like the variation in color, the broad strokes in all directions."

"Too late for flattery. Missed your chance. Get to work."

"Yes, dear. But you have to get me some more newspaper and bring me a beer."

"I guess getting out of this job is worth that."

She went to the refrigerator and opened it and got out a can of beer, popped the top. Pale Boy took the beer, sipped. "You could have left things the way they were," Pale Boy said. "The old kitchen was a lot calmer."

"Too calm."

"But look at the mess you got into."

"I knew you'd come home and save me, though I expected you a lot earlier. Bad night?"

"I'll say." Pale Boy took another swig of beer, set it on the counter, walked over to the paint can, and scraped the brush along the edge of it. The paint globbed out of it and went into the can.

"Want to talk about it?"

"Guess so."

He got down on his hands and knees, set the beer by the paint can, took the brush and began to work slowly, carefully on the edge of the counter, straightening up a thin swipe of red that looked as if someone wounded and dying had slid against it.

He began to talk. He told Angie everything he had seen, all that he knew.

"My God," Angie said. "Here in Cold Shepherd. I've never known anything like that to happen."

"Me either," Pale Boy said. "They always say more goes on in small towns than most suspect, but on the whole

I haven't found that true of Cold Shepherd. I hope this doesn't open the gate."

"The gate?"

"An expression for letting in the bad things," Pale Boy said, regretting that he had remembered one of his grandfather's expressions, and had therefore shown himself not immune to the superstitions of his past after all. "During the early sixties things weren't just peachy, never have been, but they were innocent times until John Kennedy was assassinated. After that, it was like the gate had been thrown open and a rampaging murdering horde had come through. One assassination, murder, serial killer after another. Thing I liked about this town was it seemed pretty free from even the faintest hint of that sort of thing, the craziness of Gotham, the downright drudgery of the reservation. I was wrong."

"Like I said, it surprises me, but it doesn't mean any more than what it means," Angie said. "A hit-and-run. Bad . . . horrible. But bad things are going to happen now and then, anywhere. Even Cold Shepherd. Let's just hope that's our quota of badness for a while and that you find whoever did this and lock them up."

"Lets hope."

"You're squinting. Still having headaches?"

"Yeah, some. What happened tonight didn't help any."

"You should see Catherine about it. Get a checkup."

"I will."

"Promise?"

"Sure."

"Good. I'll get that newspaper."

She went away and he took three more aspirins and had

just put the tin away when Angie came back with a bundle of paper.

While Angie watched, he arranged the newspapers around the kitchen floor and put his mind off the events of the night and concentrated on his painting. After a while the red paint was just red paint and the motions of the job worked a sort of physical hypnotism. His headache went away and he didn't notice when Angie left the room.

Some time later, she called to him from the back of the house. "Can you come here?"

"In a moment."

He paused and looked at his work. Not bad. He could clean up and stop for the night. Tomorrow he would paint the trim blue, have the whole garish job out of the way. He examined himself. He didn't even have a spatter on his uniform, his revolver, or his boots. He hadn't lost his handyman touch.

He scraped the brush clean on the edge of the paint can and put it in the can of cleaner and started to rise, but his eye caught something on one of the paint-speckled newspapers. It was a *Gotham Gazette* and it was an article about a hit-and-run in Gotham. He bent and read it.

The event had been so strange and brutal, it had made front page, and the Batman had been mentioned. He hadn't actually been involved, but he had caught a young boy who had taken a leg from one of the victims.

A leg?

Pale Boy was once again reminded of his grandfather's gate, the one that let in the bad things.

It struck him as peculiar. A hit-and-run in Gotham, and here he was investigating the same sort of crime. It seemed too coincidental.

He rose and went to the back, into Angie's studio, where the smell of paint was as strong as a blow from a baseball bat.

Angie was standing under the light looking at the painting on her easel. The light was a single naked bulb dangling down on a wire, and he couldn't understand why she didn't light her work better. She claimed it gave her the right shadow in which to view her work the way she wanted it viewed, that she painted accordingly. An eccentricity, like the mirrors she kept on the wall and sometimes used to look at her paintings, instead of examining them straight on.

She was holding a small brush in her hand, and it was dripping paint onto the already much-spattered stone floor. New colors had mixed with the red on her T-shirt, and now her face was splotched and her hair had come undone and was dangling across her forehead, over her ears, a large strand stuck to her cheek with sweat. Pale Boy thought she looked beautiful.

"What do you think?" she asked.

He examined the painting.

"Nice," he said, but didn't entirely mean it. It was a pyramid of cars. They were stacked high and it was night and the moonlight was shining through the windshields and the light looked so rich and golden it was hard to believe the effect had been accomplished by paint alone; the light appeared to be coming from a moon different from the one he knew, a moon of the netherworld.

The cars were built up with layers of paint and they stood out from the canvas in hard, crusty rust colors. They looked ancient and Gothic and full of sin, the headlights like eyes, the roofs and hoods like the shells of huge beetles. It was as if the old, bad gods had settled into the metal bones of the cars and given them a quiet, dark life and were merely biding their time until they would animate the machines and bring them down from the stack to roar and rumble about, the beams of their broken headlights sharp as glass.

It was a disconcerting painting, made all the more disconcerting by the fact that Pale Boy recognized the scene.

It wasn't just a pyramid of cars. It was a nightmarish version of *the* Pyramid of Cars that was the trademark for the reservation junkyard that had once been owned by his old man, Billy Hands.

Strangeness washed over Pale Boy. Angie knew, of course, that he had been born and raised on the reservation, but he had never mentioned his father had owned the famous Pyramid of Cars junkyard, or that now his brother Abner owned it. Or he assumed he still owned it, as he himself had relinquished all claim to it, therefore making Abner the next in line to receive it.

But the more he thought about the painting, the less strange he felt. It wasn't so coincidental after all, or so he told himself. The pyramid had become a famous landmark in these parts. It was visible from the road and Angie had seen it, as anyone who passed by the reservation on their way to Cold Shepherd or Gotham might see it, and now she was painting it from memory, adding her own dark and inspired touches.

Still, with what had happened tonight, the hit-and-run, the blood-red paint, the article in the *Gotham Gazette*, the strange waking dream of a boy hanging, and now the painting, it gave him the creeps. Too much congruence. It made the old head wound hurt again. It made him remember what his grandfather, Jerome Horse Handler, had taught him and his brother. A lesson he had tried to forget, along with most of his Indian lessons—lessons that he now thought pagan and silly, lessons that gave too much power to coincidence. One lesson went, "Never ignore a collection of signs. The Old Ones are trying to tell you something."

But even as he dismissed these things, he remembered another. The owl he had seen in the alley. He recalled he had been taught to fear its moonlit shadow, for it represented the Owl God, and in its fleeting darkness was supposedly housed the very essence of mortality, and to be touched by it was to be touched by the hand of death.

9

1:00 A.M.

Pale Boy lay awake beside Angie, trying to will himself to sleep, but it was useless. He had drifted off for a while, but his head had soon filled with the vision of the hanging boy, and this time the dream was in better focus. The boy's noose was not a rope, but a twist of colored automotive wiring. He could see the boy's face in the dream, and it was shaded with shadow, but somehow familiar, familiar like a melody heard long ago and faintly remembered, one you can no longer put a name to.

Then he awoke, feeling fearful and confused. The dream was gone, but now, awake, he kept remembering Martha and Evan and the multiple strangeness of the day. To worsen matters, his head hurt.

He was almost delighted when the phone rang.

Angie made a noise like someone eating paper, and Pale Boy rolled quickly from beneath the covers and padded into the living room to grab the phone on the third ring. It was Catherine Meadows.

"Know it's late, but I figured you couldn't go right to bed after what we saw tonight," she said. "God knows I couldn't sleep— Damn, I forgot about Angie."

"It's all right. She didn't wake up and I couldn't sleep anyway."

"I just wanted to tell you Evan has gone from bad to worse, and I'm having him moved by ambulance to Gotham Memorial. I thought you'd want to know."

"Thanks, Catherine."

"You're welcome, and good night."

He hung up, went to the kitchen and drank a glass of milk, then returned to the living room. He turned on the end table light, plucked one of the books from the shelf, sat on the couch, and tried to read.

Normally that would have been the thing. Books, even bad ones, rested his soul. He not only delighted in his ability to consume words like candy, but the very act of reading made him secure. It reminded him that he had pulled himself up by his bootstraps, and he was proud of that. He had come from an illiterate family, and he had barely learned to read and write at the reservation school, and neither his father or his mother (in the little time he knew her) took any interest in books or their contents. But when he entered the army years later and saw that the more educated a man was the faster he made rank, he went to work on improving himself. Got a little help from a reading tutor on base, then set himself the task of consuming more books, learning everything he could from them, found it wasn't only beneficial, it was also interesting and fun.

Turned out it didn't help his army career, since it was

shortened by that drunk's hitting him on the head, but the quality of his life went up several notches because of it, and he had never stopped reading. Everything from Poe to Melville to John Cheever to Robert F. Jones, the philosophers and historians.

But tonight the words were symbols without any meaning he could decipher. He would have had as much luck trying to read a volume written in Sanskrit.

Returning the book to the shelf, he switched on the television and attempted to watch an old black and white movie. But he couldn't keep his mind on it, and his thoughts kept drifting to what he had seen in the street earlier, to the owl's shadow floating over his head, and to Angie's painting.

He turned off the television, went into Angie's study, pulled the string that switched on the light, examined the painting and felt a chill moving from the back of his heels up to his neck.

He was uncertain why a painting of such a familiar place as the Pyramid of Cars should have this effect on him. It made absolutely no sense. His father had built the pyramid himself with a crane and welding torch. He had thought it would be great advertisement for his junkyard, as it could be seen from the road and would be more interesting than just a bunch of gutted and rusted cars parked at random in the large lot by the road. The old man sometimes referred to the Pyramid of Cars as his personal tepee, though the Manowacks had never lived in that type of structure, and Pale Boy's father knew it.

Pale Boy remembered when he was eight, awakening mornings in the bed he shared with his older brother, and looking out of their cracked and taped bedroom window glass and seeing, at the far edge of the car lot, the back of the pyramid. It seemed strange in the early morning sunlight. The dew glistened on it as if phosphorescent. It looked ancient and mystical then. From the rear, the opening his father had made into the pyramid (Pale Boy could never bring himself to call it a tepee) was visible and dark and somehow foreboding, like the lair of some mythological beast that feasted on boys his age.

Pale Boy knew there was nothing inside the pyramid but a chair and a small fold-out table, but the looks of the thing bothered him anyway. When business was bad, which was most of the time, his father would sit inside the pyramid at the table and deal out useless hand after hand of solitaire and sip from a bottle of whiskey. He'd sip until he felt better or worse.

When he drank and shuffled cards, the family laid low. You never knew what might cause the old man to have an explosion, never knew what might bring him out from there with his belt off, beating not only Pale Boy and his brother, but their mother as well.

Other times, the old man abandoned the pyramid to sit atop the car crusher in the rusted cab and work the gears as if he were a fighter pilot maneuvering in a dogfight. He was joyful then. You could see it on his face. He delighted in the pulsing and rattling of the great crusher, and he delighted in seeing the junk cars sliding into the cradle and in working the levers that would make the machinery squeak and turn the once mighty road machines into little square metal boxes that could be sold for scrap.

His father's life was cars. He had discovered them as a child and had made them his business, his life, and his dream. There was a magic in them, his father always said. A way to be gone from places you hated. You need only put gas in them and go.

But his old man had not gone far. He drove about the reservation and sometimes into the smaller outlaying towns and once into Gotham, but the great city traffic had terrified him and he had never gone back. He always said that for it to really matter, you had to have the right engine, one that would carry you away and keep you away; maybe something like a V-8 Thunderbird with good tires and a heater that worked, a good spare in the trunk.

As a boy, it confused Pale Boy, but he knew now what had kept Billy Hands tied to the reservation. It was the family he both loved and hated. Loved because they were his blood, hated because they held him to a land where he had been born and his father had been born and his grandfather had been born, and where the entire Manowack tribe had once been great before the arrival of whites and smallpox and cheap whiskey; a land whose best promise was varying degrees of poverty.

Strangely enough, it was his mother, Evelyn, who had lived their father's dreams. She had run off in a big, finned Cadillac with a white shoe salesman with oiled-down hair and a smile full of gold fillings. The salesman came in to look at used cars one day, talked Cadillacs, then spied Evelyn. He stuck around to eat beans and cornbread with the family, talked Cadillacs some more, and then the whiskey came out of his shoe sales case (his name, Jerry Heilman, was stenciled in gold on the top of it next to the handle) and he and Billy Hands nipped at it until Billy passed out beneath the table. This left the salesman and

Evelyn, Pale Boy, and Abner. Mom and the salesman looked at one another and smiled and Mom sent Pale Boy and Abner off to bed.

That was the last thing Pale Boy remembered of either salesman or his mother. The family never saw either again, but two years after her parting they got a box with two pairs of boy's shoes in it that fit neither of their feet, and a late Christmas card. The postmark showed shoes and card had been mailed from someplace in Wyoming. The card said, "Just wanted to check in."

She never checked in after that, but the salesman sent a note to them a year later from Vermont. It informed them that their mother, Evelyn, had taken to drinking and died. Their father read them the note and never mentioned his wife again. He turned even harder to the bottle and more to the car crusher, producing countless little metal boxes, diminishing heavy cars that might have been sold as running junkers. But the money no longer mattered to the old man. What mattered was the feeling of power he got from the crusher and the no-competition card game he played. These were the only times he felt the world was his to control and outside influences didn't matter. If he failed to have self-worth, he at least had power of a sort. When he dealt the cards he dealt little fates; when he pulled the levers on the crusher, he put all his fears and hates and losses into the vibrations of the machine, the pulling and pushing of the levers, the sounds of the ill-fated cars shape-shifting from fuel-powered carriages to boxes of scrap.

His father's other measure of power, the beatings, stopped, however, and Pale Boy had strangely been bothered by that. It was, except for one piece of advice his father gave them—"Get off this reservation, and stay off.

Be white as you can be''—the end of any real communication between himself and his father, and it was then that he and his brother turned to their grandfather.

Thinking of that now, Pale Boy felt an overwhelming urge to return to the reservation and see the old places. It was the first time he had even considered such a thing since leaving the Manowack lands to join the white world. It surprised him, but the need would not pass.

He put on his clothes and wrote Angie a note: *Be back soon.* He got the keys to his pickup and went quietly out the back door and locked it. He got in the pickup and sat for a moment, trying to talk himself out of what he planned to do, but could not. He looked about the interior of the ragged old Ford and smiled to himself. If his denying his Indian heritage and leaving the reservation was his liberation from the Manowack and his grandfather, then this truck was his liberation from his father and his passion for cars. It ran, but it was nothing special; he was no longer tied to jacked-up rear ends and rich upholstery. He was free of both brands of shackles.

He cranked the engine, backed out of the carport, and drove out of Cold Shepherd, set the nose of the truck for the reservation. The pirate-ship moon still rode cool and high in the sky and the shadows of the great trees along the highway flicked across his windshield like the cards his father had dealt so long ago, flipping them out like a god dealing doom.

When he reached the reservation lands, saw the great Pyramid of Cars atop the hill, standing tall and exotic in the moonlight, looking for all the world as foreboding as Angie's painting, he pulled across the highway and backed the truck so that he was facing it and the Cadillac billboard.

The billboard was positioned out and below the Pyramid of Cars, and from pyramid to billboard was a long slanting drop. As a child, he often sat atop the pyramid with his brother, and they tossed rocks at the back of the sign, their tosses invariably falling far short of their aim.

The billboard had been there since he was a little boy, and, for whatever reason, had never been changed. It had faded considerably. It was a large painting of a man's head wearing a cowboy hat and glasses. The man was smiling. There was a cartoon-style balloon coming out of the man's mouth, and written in the balloon was, BUY CADILLAC. IT'LL MAKE YOU HAPPY TO DRIVE. Above that, written in even larger letters, was, BARRETT'S CADILLACS, THE PLACE TO BUY AND SAVE.

When Pale Boy was young, and the beatings were intense, he sometimes ran away from his father and hid here. Back then there had been a thick clutch of bushes to conceal and warm him. He would sit and look through a split in the bushes and see the billboard and take in the painted smile of the man—Barrett, he presumed. Somehow the sign reassured him. He thought when he grew up he'd buy a Cadillac from Barrett, drive it around the reservation for everyone to see, then drive off to a nice house somewhere in the suburbs of Gotham where a good-looking white wife waited for him with dinner on the table.

But now he looked at the faded billboard and thought only of how bad things had been, remembered his grandfather, and felt guilty. Unlike his father, his grandfather, Jerome Horse Handler, had hated the whites and all they stood for. He was the last in a long line of shamans, and his son, Pale Boy's father, Billy Hands, had rejected the old ways and had learned nothing of them.

What Billy Hands had passed on to his sons was not the study of the wind, rain, sun, and animals, but instead the study of Fords, Chevys, Pontiacs, and Buicks, the fin sizes of old Cadillacs, the sturdiness of Lincolns, the dependability and longevity of their old man's Holy Grail of automobiles, the '57 Thunderbird.

Billy Hand's personal magic was in the car magazines he collected and cluttered about the tiny shack, magazines that Pale Boy and his brother read when they were sad and lonely and frightened, magazines with glossy jacked-up cars painted cherry red and glitter blue, bathing-suited beauties draped over their hoods like ornamental rugs.

At night, while their father drank himself into a stupor in front of the snowy TV set topped with sagging rabbit ears, he and Abner could put their heads together beneath the covers and with a flashlight examine the contents of the magazines and enter a fantasy land where the bright cars with the cocked behinds and the chrome trim were not photos and paper but the real thing, and they, the Indian dreamers, were not under the covers but behind the steering wheels, cruising with the bathing beauties at their sides. In truth, they were too young to know exactly what the near naked women were all about. They only knew that they looked good, and somehow looking at them made them feel simultaneously comfortable and miserable inside, a feeling not too unlike the one they felt while looking at the photos of the cars.

"Udden, udden," his older brother would say.

When Billy Hands took completely to the bottle, the cards, and the car crusher, Pale Boy and his brother Abner took to drawing the cars in the magazines. They drew them on paper sacks with stubby pencils while listening to music on their ragged record player. Both player and records had been given them by a female social worker one Christmas. They had belonged to the social worker's children and were well used, the records scratchy, mostly hot rod rock 'n' roll music by the Beach Boys, Jan & Dean, a few others, but they sounded like a heavenly choir to Pale Boy and Abner.

The boys listened to the records over and over, and even the normally quarrelsome Billy Hands seemed to enjoy the music, as long as the songs they played were the car songs.

Eventually Billy Hands left them completely to their own devices. They took to eating at the houses of friends and hanging out with their grandfather, Jerome Horse Handler, a strange old man who wandered in and out of the mountains and came by to see them from time to time, but never spoke a word to his grease monkey son, Billy Hands.

Billy referred to Jerome as "that old Indian bastard," as if he himself were of a different origin, perhaps the virgin birth of some wandering God-blessed white woman.

Jerome Horse Handler, on the rare occasions he used English, called his son Uncle Tomahawk and worse. They had even once come to blows, with the boys' ancient grandfather handling the stronger Billy Hands with the ease of a grizzly swatting a coyote. The old man seemed to know everything Billy was going to do before he did it. He whipped Billy without ever hitting him. He merely dodged and pushed and sidestepped and sent Billy reeling to the ground so many times he began to look natural there in the dust.

When the fight was over, Billy disappeared into the

pyramid, and after a time, they heard the slapping of the cards, punctuated by sporadic cursing.

Until that time, they had only known their grandfather to be this ancient, leathery personage with long white hair and a goofy set of clothes.

Slowly it dawned on Pale Boy and Abner that they might not in fact be akin to the TV cowboys they played from time to time, but the descendants of the less fortunate Indians, the guys who were always sneaking up on white men and shooting them from ambush, raping the women and stealing the horses. Not exactly the role models they had in mind.

In time, Pale Boy and his brother went to live with their grandfather in his little tarpaper shack in the mountains of the reservation. The shack was even simpler than their father's home, and much smaller. They slept on mats on the dirt floor and ate what their grandfather raised and hunted. They were introduced to the old ways, the magic ways. No rock 'n' roll and no cars.

In time, Pale Boy and Abner learned that their grandfather was a reservation legend. He was rumored to be well over a hundred years old. It was said he fathered Billy Hands when he was in his eighties and his fifth wife was in her thirties.

Pale Boy had no way to confirm any of this, but it was obvious the old man was held in high regard by the Manowacks, even if no one on the reservation seemed to be in a rush to live the life he was living, the one he said was the only one they should live. Pale Boy could understand their reluctance. The mountains were beautiful, and so were the birds and animals that lived there, but in the winter the mountains were cold, and so was their grandfather's shack. It made their father's old house seem like a palace. And there were no cars to look at, no magazines to dream over, no music to tap your foot to. The pursuit of food and warmth was, to put it mildly, one that provided regular exercise.

Pale Boy learned in time that his grandmother had died in childbirth bringing his father into the world. Jerome often said that had he known his only remaining son (three of the others had already fed their livers to alcohol and a fourth had been struck by a car while drunkenly trying to cross the highway) was going to turn out the way he had, he wouldn't have bothered to help conceive him. If he had his choice between the boy and his last wife, he said, he would have given up Billy for the woman.

The old man taught them the boys' chants and showed them the holy places on the mountain and in the valley, and sometimes late at night they would go up to the high curve, as it was known among the tribe, and walk out to its edge and gaze below. Down there they could see the moonlit wrecking yard and the Pyramid of Cars. The cars on the lot were as small as snails. Farther out, and down a stretch from the wrecking yard, the back of the billboard was visible and no larger than a postage stamp.

Jerome Horse Handler would point to the highway beyond the sign, at the headlights speeding along like jet-propelled fireflies, and say, "There is the end of the Manowacks. In the white man's engines. We are losing the old ways. It is not the white man that fears being captured by the injuns these days, it is the red man who should fear being captured by the white man's engines. They are sucking out our soul. They're filling our air with stink.

The grass and trees on the sides of the mountains near the highways are dying from the coughing of the machines. The whole world is going mad. The sacred animals, the wolf, the owl, they are fewer and fewer, and where once they were strong and brave and noble, they are now pathetic shadows of what they once were. They have become highway scavengers. Their nobility is drying up. Just like the Manowacks who once worshiped them."

Then he would take them to a higher place and they would strip off their clothes and Jerome Horse Handler would build a fire of hickory and sassafras and pine, would toss herbs and charms into the fire and chant the old words. The smoke would fill their nostrils, the chants would fill their brains. They would sit across from Jerome Horse Handler and he would raise an arm and wave, as if signaling to something beyond the earthly realm. When he lowered his arm, it would be covered with fur and his hand would be a large paw. Then the smoke would grow thick and shield him from view. When it blew aside, there would stand a great gray wolf. It would lift its head to the stars and howl.

Pale Boy remembered his brother learning to do the same as Jerome, to shape-shift into animals and birds, and remembered even more dimly doing it himself, running through the forest as a wolf, flying above the mountains as a hawk.

He didn't believe these memories, thought perhaps they had been induced by something hallucinogenic in the smoke, caused by the "charms" his grandfather tossed into the fire. But there were times when the memory of the owl's intense night sight and the wolf's marvelous sense of smell seemed as real a recollection as tonight's hit-and-run horror.

When Pale Boy was nine he left his grandfather. He missed the cars too much, and Jerome Horse Handler had become harder and harder to live with. The old ways had deserted him. There were no more mountain smokes. He said he had lost the power, that the white man's powers had invaded the otherworlds and he no longer understood what was expected of him. The spirits had left him high and dry.

Abner had lost the power, too, and it was then that Pale Boy began to doubt any of them had ever possessed it. He left his grandfather and went back to his father and the car magazines. But his brother wouldn't come. He stayed. He wanted the old ways, even though the old man no longer seemed able to teach them.

His father was neither glad nor disappointed to see him. He was too deep in the bottle. Pale Boy took up with Billy Hands where he had left off. No obvious demonstrations of love. No beatings. Billy treated him at least as well as he treated strangers, and there were lots of car magazines to read and the old records to listen to.

Jerome Horse Handler died not long after Pale Boy returned to the lot, and the story went that Abner, as per his grandfather's request, pulled the old man's body to the top of a tree and left it there for the vultures. Abner came back to the lot then, but he had changed, and he and Pale Boy were no longer close. Abner treated him like a deserter. Pale Boy had become even paler to him—he was the Invisible Man.

Then one cold morning Billy Hands finished off a bottle

of rotgut, played a hand of solitaire, rigged the car crusher with an automatic switch, crawled into a mud-colored Thunderbird, and allowed himself to be wenched into position and crushed.

The neighbors helped Pale Boy bury Billy. The metal block that contained him was interred in a cardboard box in a shallow grave out back of the house. A hubcap was put up in the dirt to mark the spot. Pale Boy honked a horn on one of the better cars and poured a can of thirty weight on the grave and wished him clear highways and a red Thunderbird convertible. Abner didn't show up for the burying.

Actually, Pale Boy didn't remember much about Abner after that time. There seemed to be a blank in his head. He could recall that Abner hated him for abandoning their grandfather, but not much else. He remembered staying with an aunt for a time, then a series of uncles. Nothing special about any of that. No one took him under his or her wing. They merely made sure he had a place to get in out of the rain and three squares a day, and not all of them that square.

When he was old enough, he left the reservation and followed his old man's advice about trying to be white. He thought the military would be a good start. He joined up, was shipped to a base in Virginia, became an M.P., mostly forgot about cars and Indian magic, came back to the Great Gotham Valley a few years back, thinking his life as an Indian was over.

Now here he was again, right back where he had come from, back with the billboard and the Pyramid of Cars.

And a headache.

He looked up at the pyramid and noted for the first time that there was something at its tip. It looked like a chair, or more accurately, a throne.

Abner—that would be his work. He would like that. A throne where he could sit and watch the cars on the highway go by, as if they were his subjects.

He wondered what Abner was doing tonight. Sleeping in the old shack, in their old bedroom, maybe listening to the scratchy rock 'n' roll records? Sighing over the blond bathing beauties draped over the hoods of sparkling automobiles? Watching cowboy and Indian movies on the tube, the way their father had? Or perhaps he really had given up the white ways and was on the floor, drawing in the dust with a stick, working Indian magic, still trying to change into a wolf, trying to live their grandfather's lies, capture his illusions.

Pale Boy examined the luminous face of his watch. Two twenty-five. He took two aspirin from the tin and chewed them, rolled the truck window down and leaned back in his seat, and looked at the Cadillac sign, at Barrett's smile, felt urges he couldn't identify. He ceased trying. He closed his eyes and drifted off to sleep, dreamed briefly of the hanging boy, then dreamed not at all.

Clutch and Shift to—

—Second Gear

1

Gotham City, the Bowery, 2:25 A.M.

The place was nasty. The streets were full of trash, the buildings tight against one another, their shadows claustrophobic.

The buildings themselves contained little or no light and they were barred up and many were empty and boarded over. Occasionally, inside, there would be the flicker of fires where drifters had broken in and made themselves a camp for the night, but mostly they were dark. The air was full of the smell of alcohol and urine and the burning of steel wool pads for heating up and making crack. Drunks and fugitives made their way down the sidewalks, staying close to the buildings and the shadows. Somewhere in that little warren called the Bowery, crimes were being committed with the casualness of a teenager chewing gum. You listened close enough you could hear a crowbar snapping wood somewhere in the distance, smell a whiff of smoke from a fire being set for insurance money. In winter, a warm air vent and a slug of wine in a discarded bottle were plenty of incentive for violence, even murder. In summer, the heat, held tight between bricks and concrete, intensified by smog and desperation, could work some people up to a kill.

So-called decent people stayed indoors behind a variety of locks with loaded pistols in their nightstands, shotguns and rifles stuffed under their beds. If someone out on the street screamed for help, best thing they could do was put a pillow over their head so they couldn't hear it. General wisdom was, you went out there when bad things were happening, bad things would happen to you too.

On this sticky night in July, dead center of the Bowery, walking slowly, weakly, a baby in her arms, came a once cute blond woman freshly turned twenty, but living experience-wise on the far side of forty. Her name was Mandy and she was thirteen months off the bus from Nebraska. She was carrying her baby girl, Kerrie.

Thirteen months ago she had come from the flatlands to the modern badlands, not knowing it was that way, seeing only the allure of lights and action and a big time job. Hoping for distance between her and her deeply religious parents. Religious except in the compassion department, that is.

After graduation from high school, she had been a secretary back in Nebraska for her minister father's church, and a good one at that, but her secretarial career lacked the glamour she wanted. Adding up one night's worth of church offerings was not too unlike adding up two nights.

Checking the church rolls to see who was coming to Bible classes and who had dropped out was no greater thrill. Three or four minutes of that kind of work and the heart ceased to beat with excitement.

At the houses of friends she had seen some of the life she wanted on television. Visions denied her at home, where the tube was tuned only to religious programs, preachers in peach-colored and lime-colored suits with bone-white shoes and hair stiff as plastic caps.

She had seen some of this desired life in her friends' magazines as well. Magazines she was denied at home. There she had only the hardline religious magazines with non-gloss covers featuring the preachers she saw on television, their faces beaded with the sweat of salvation, their arms outstretched, hands wide open, as if groping for money.

What she saw in her friends' magazines were different. Bright fashions where women showed their legs and rouged their cleavage, took taxis downtown and ate in restaurants by candlelight.

So she slipped away from her parents one night. Away from their porcelain statues of Jesus, their paintings of martyred saints with their flesh full of arrows, and went to Gotham—called by her parents the city of sin—to find her fortune.

But fortune in Gotham proved a little short in supply. She discovered there were already plenty of good secretaries in Gotham, and the fast-food joints were full-up with pimple-faced kids taking orders for burgers, drinks and fries. Jobs of any kind were rarer than smiles.

A month after she was off the bus, she concluded she hadn't had it so bad back in Nebraska. She came to wish she had just moved out of her parents' house and found an apartment in her home town. Acquired a new job.

But in her darkest hour, things abruptly looked up. The proverbial silver lining in the proverbial dark cloud revealed itself. She met a nice man who helped her out. He gave her smiles and he gave her money. He rented her an apartment, said just as soon as he could get that doggone divorce from his wife, he was going to marry her. He gave her lots of things. And one night, he gave her the seed that fertilized her egg. Her belly swelled up and the nice man gave her money for six months rent, then found pressing business elsewhere, but he said there would be more money, and he'd be back.

After his departure, no money came. She began to live off the rent money. She tried to get a job, but jobs were no more available than before. She couldn't afford day care. The money the nice man had given her for her apartment ran out, and apparently, the nice man's business proved more pressing than he had indicated. Couple months later, he finally came by to say things had improved at home and he and the wife were patching it up. He said that the name Mandy knew him by was a lie, and he regretted that, and he was certainly a stinker, but he thought it best if she didn't know his real name. Then or now.

As a parting gift, he gave her a couple of thousand and a kiss on the cheek. She stood in the doorway of the apartment with the money in her hand, stunned. The nice man hadn't asked about the baby, how the pregnancy was going. He waved good-bye from the end of the hall, as if she were a child he were sending off to school. She never saw him again.

The baby arrived about the time the first half of the nice man's money played out. People at the welfare office were understanding. They said money would come through for her and the baby eventually. After a couple of months, Mandy decided eventually meant about the time her baby was old enough to work.

It hurt, but she decided to crawl. Called her parents and told them her plight. Her father's voice made her cry. She felt a glow of love and warmth swell through her when he said hello. She begged for forgiveness. Said she loved him, and meant it. Said he was now a grandfather to a beautiful baby girl.

He said he didn't think so. They told her she wasn't welcome at home. That she was a whore, and must get right with The Almighty and that she was no longer their daughter, though, as was befitting of those who trusted in His mercy, they wished her the best, and they preferred she not call again.

Mandy decided she wanted to go back to Nebraska anyway. She knew the people there and she knew the way of life. She wanted to get a job, any job, and do right by her child. But Nebraska seemed to have grown farther away than before. There wasn't any money to go home. There wasn't any money for much of anything, and she was amazed to discover how regularly the body craved food. Glamour had fallen off the top of her desire list. Food had moved right up there. Gotham's lights didn't warm her and the city's action didn't thrill her. Gotham was in a very short time a place of brutal sound, harsh light and emptiness. A city of millions who moved like wraiths from one street to the other; a place thick with souls that never touched.

Her nice apartment in Glendale was beyond her means. The only place she could afford was a room in the Bowery. It was like living in hell, minus the benefits. That wasn't bad enough, she got so she couldn't afford the room. The landlord said he hated to see her go, but business was business, and wasn't that baby cute.

Home for awhile was a fire escape, a cardboard box with all the trimmings. But a bad rain had melted her box, and home now was wherever she found herself.

To sustain she took to the streets, found her survival with men in back alleys and abandoned buildings, taking what money they offered, and sometimes getting none, but instead a fist in the mouth or a hard shove-down. She associated with the homeless, the riff-raff and the drug pushers.

Things got bad after that. And now, tonight, they seemed about as bad as they could get.

An hour ago, she had almost put a needle full of junk in her arm. It had been offered to her in lieu of payment for her services rendered.

Only the cries of her child had prevented her from taking a trip to the gritty promiseland where nothing mattered but the bad come down and the next go up.

But Kerrie's cries had pulled her back into the real world and onto the street, and now here she was, hot and hungry and the baby crying again. She felt as if she had to keep walking, right on out of the Bowery, right across Gotham, across the heartland of America, on back to Nebraska where she could find an old school friend, sleep one night in a warm bed with clean sheets, eat a meal that wasn't out of a garbage can, give her body enough nutrients to produce more than a trickle of breast milk for Kerrie. Maybe she could even convince her parents to take her in. She had been taught to believe in miracles.

Yeah, just walk on back to Nebraska. But she couldn't walk that far. She couldn't even walk out of the Bowery tonight. She had to find a place to sleep, and the baby needed food and so did she.

Suddenly she lost her thoughts. Her vision was full of Leather Boys.

It was as if they had grown up out of the street's pavement: six guys in their fabled attire of black leather vests and multicolored, patchwork leather pants made from fragments taken from stolen wallets and worn-out jackets, chunks scrounged from garbage and dump sights, slashed from car seats upholstered in real leather. Six guys with smiles that winked in the moonlight like sharp blades.

The blood thumped in Mandy's temples. She stopped. Of all the street horrors to run into, the Leather Boys were one of the worst. Even during her short time on the street, she had heard of them. A gang made up of dopeheads so vile other gangs and street muggers considered them the lowest scum on the Bowery totem pole. They were the scavengers of the gang world. Not brave, but deadly. Worked the Bowery turf on the sly, when they thought all the real gangs were out of it for the night. That's when the Leather Boys came out and took the leavings, stole from the homeless and kicked sleeping winos to death for sport, or poured gasoline on them and set them on fire, cooked some stolen marshmallows in the flames. She'd heard all the stories. But until now, she thought they might be a myth.

She was about twenty feet from them when one of the guys said, "Hey, honey, you're clicking along in a hurry."

She didn't say anything. Nothing seemed appropriate.

"You're that friendly girly, ain't you?" the same guy said. "One's working our turf for the lay and pay. Am I right on that? Someone comes in here new, eventually the Leather Boys hear about it, you know?"

The sleeping baby stirred on Mandy's shoulder, made a wimpering noise, settled back to sleep. She looked at the six guys standing there, felt her knees going weak, but something her father told her long ago came to her. "You ever get a pack a dogs after you, don't run. You run, they're gonna smell fear and they'll take you down for sure. You do better to stand your ground and bluff till you can do different."

She smiled and said, "I'm friendly when I want to be, but I don't want to be now. I got to get the baby home. I do that, I can come back. But you know, it'll cost a bit."

The same guy pursed his lips and studied a spot just over her head. "Cost a little bit, huh?"

Play cool, she thought. *Play cool*. "Yeah. I'm worth it."

The guy turned to his friends, cocked a thumb in her direction, said to the boys, "Says she's worth it." He turned back to her. "You know, thing I heard was you get something that's worth something for free, it's worth a whole lot more. Know what I'm saying?"

She tried to play it cool, unafraid. "Yeah, but I got the baby with me."

"Hey, that don't bother us none." He turned to the others. "That bother us?"

They shook their heads. Nobody looked bothered.

He turned back to Mandy. "See, there's no problem here. We can even take the brat off your hands. There's people will buy a kid like that. Give him a better home than you can. We know about you. You ain't got no home to go to. Word on the street is you ain't got nothing to go to."

"Enough chitchat," said one of the other guys.

"Yeah," said the one who had been talking. "Enough chitchat."

Mandy stood frozen. If she fought, the baby could get hurt. There seemed nothing to do but to take it, and then hope for a break, a chance to get the baby back.

They were right in front of her now, forming a loose circle. Her legs quivered, lost their muscle. She dropped to her knees.

Then came a voice from the dark, a voice like God calling to Moses: "Don't."

"Hey," said the one who talked the most. "Who said that?" He squinted into the shadows. "You come out where we can see you. We got some things we want to show you."

As if by secret signal, the Leather Boys flexed their hands and knives appeared.

"Come on," said the head Leather Boy. "Talk tough, now."

Mandy stared through a gap in the Leather Boys, in

the shadowy direction from which she thought the voice had come. The spot she was watching moved. The shadow coiled and flowed, looked like a ball of night rolling into view. It was the swish of a cloak being thrown back, revealing a tall, dark demon with pointed ears. The demon moved again and she saw it was a man, and suddenly she knew who he was. She had read about him in Nebraska, seen grainy newspaper photographs of him. Like the Leather Boys, she half thought he was a myth.

"Hot damn!" said a Leather Boy. "The Batman!"

"He ain't nothing," said the main talker. "Just some guy in a suit. There's enough of us to take him."

"Start the dance," Batman said.

"You talk big," said the main Leather Boy. "We hear about you coming down here, messing in the Bowery business. Well, you haven't seen us before, the Leather Boys. Mess with us once, you don't mess again."

Batman took a step forward. Shadows appeared to scuttle at his feet and around his head. His cloak swirled, like a shaggy rip of darkness. Now that he was out of the thickest of the shadows, Mandy saw that the lower half of his face was not covered by his mask, and as he moved to dead center of the street, the dust-filmed streetlight fell full on him, and she saw him smile. He looked rabid.

The head Leather Boy spun his knife like a miniature baton. The blade gathered in the light, fanned it, then dropped it.

Batman glided toward the thug. The movement was so smooth it was like watching a specter pass over the earth.

The punk leapt forward, right leg going out and bending deep, his right arm jabbing straight and true, the blade speeding forward so fast it looked like a laser beam, heading directly toward the symbol of the light-encased bat on Batman's chest.

When the tip of the knife was a fraction of an inch away and the Leather Boy was already congratulating himself, Batman swiveled to the side and the blade passed by. Batman's arm went out like a whip and he used the side of his hand to strike the Leather Boy across the nose. The nose erupted blood and the Leather Boy screamed. Batman's leg flashed, the top of his foot striking the thug low on the calf, stunning the nerves there so severely the Leather Boy collapsed with a yell and lay in the street holding his leg. Batman kicked him in the face, knocking him unconscious.

Batman was a machine now. He moved sure and certain, the reptilian brain at work.

One of the remaining five sprang forward, slashing with his knife. The slash was slow and wild, not even close. Batman shot out his right leg, catching his attacker in the throat with the upturned heel. The Leather Boy dropped his knife and brought both hands to his throat and collapsed to his knees, toppled on his side with a cough.

Batman recoiled his leg, whipped it back and around and caught the elbow of his next attacker with a heel kick. The elbow snapped and the attacker screamed. Batman sidestepped into him with a thrust kick that launched him onto the sidewalk, where he spun on his butt like a break dancer, then collapsed unconscious.

A knife flashed from behind Batman, but it was as if

he had eyes in the back of his head. He moved slightly, letting the blade slip by. Then he was turning, catching the knife arm at the elbow, twisting it until it snapped; then, with another twist, he sent the thug flying across the street and slamming into a building wall. The Leather Boy slid down the bricks and crunched to the ground like a hunk of wet garbage.

The remaining two rushed Batman simultaneously, one on the left, one on the right. Batman dodged back, put out a foot. The right-hand Leather Boy tripped and lurched forward into the other, hitting him knee-high and knocking him down.

Immediately Batman was on them, fists and knees and elbows thrashing, and during the blinking of an eye, Mandy realized it was all over. The six lay on the ground, all of them with broken bones and shattered spirits, moaning or unconscious. Batman looked around, as if hoping for more adversaries, appeared slightly disappointed when none appeared.

He gathered up his attackers' knives, and one by one put the blades beneath the heel of his boot and snapped them. Finished, he turned and looked at Mandy. She felt a new sort of terror. What if she was next? What if he was crazy as a loon?

He walked toward her, extended his hand. She made sure her grip on Kerrie was secure, reached up with her free hand, and took his. He pulled her to her feet. "It's all right," he said.

He was different now, his body language reassuring. She felt weak but comfortable, safe for the first time in ages. She fell against him and he put an arm around her and Kerrie. The baby squirmed, cried softly, and was still again.

"I'm so alone," Mandy said.

"I know," he said, and somehow she knew he did. She cried into his chest, her tears dampening the insignia on his uniform.

2

Parking Lot Outside Gotham Memorial Hospital, 3:00 A.M.

The young man slipped through the shrubs and entered the far side of the hospital parking lot and looked in the direction the grounds guard had taken, said to himself, "Only thing that dude could guard is a box of doughnuts. Some coffee, maybe."

He walked along a row of parked cars, looking, stopped by a nice new Ford, and reached into his pants pocket. He had neatly cut the bottom out of the pocket back when the pants were new for just this sort of thing. He reached through the hole and took hold of the crowbar that was strapped to his leg inside a leather holster.

He looked around. No one in sight.

He pulled the bar out and walked to the trunk of the Ford and stuck the bar into the crack between trunk and frame and heaved hard, once. The lock snapped. The trunk lid sprang up.

He put the crowbar back in its place and reached inside the trunk and undid the screw that held the spare tire, heaved out the tire, leaned it against the car, and closed the lid of the trunk. He took a roll of electrician's tape from his other pocket and taped the broken trunk lid down to the frame with two quick swipes and tears of the tape. By the time the car's owner figured out the tire was gone, he wouldn't have any idea where or when it was stolen.

He took hold of the tire, turned, and looked back at the hospital just as the fourth-floor wall exploded bricks and glass and the front end of a black Thunderbird poked out into the night, its headlight beams looking as bright and firm as gold-painted planks. The car bent its front as if made of rubber, dipped its headlights, placed its tires on the outside wall of the hospital, revved its motor, and slid forward. It looked like the building was giving birth to it. The headlight beams hit the ground, gave the impression of support, like slowly dissolving stanchions. Insects found the beams and fluttered in their light.

Down went the Thunderbird, the front tires rolling and molding softly with the outside wall, tugging the rest of the dark car after them until the back tires cleared the gap in the building. On all four tires it crept like a housefly, the tires actually extending forward cartoonlike, *stepping*, clinging to the brick. Then it was reaching for the earth, stretching, the front tires touching the ground, the humming motor urging the rest of the car away from the wall so that it was on all fours again, rolling swiftly. Its radio began blaring, "Little Deuce Coupe," then it hit the exit and was gone, the music dangling behind it like something being dragged.

"Now, that's seriously different," said the thief. He hadn't seen stuff like that even when he was sniffing glue.

He looked down and saw that the eruption of brick and glass had gotten the guard's attention away from his doughnuts or whatever. He was running around the building with his gun drawn.

The thief rolled the tire smoothly and briskly, shoved it through the hedges, jumped them, caught up with the tire before it could get off the walkway. He used his hand to keep it going. He rolled it around the corner and off the walk to his pickup. He grabbed it without slowing and tossed it with a grunt into the truck bed with the other tires he'd stolen. It had been a good night.

He opened the passenger door and flung himself inside. He reached the key from his shirt pocket, slid over to the driver's side, stuck the key in the ignition and smiled, then quit smiling.

Nothing happened when he turned the key. Not a burp.

He eased out of the truck and opened the hood.

Someone had stolen the battery and starter while he had been in the parking lot, and the whole job hadn't taken him more than five minutes.

"Now ain't that hell," he said aloud. It was getting so the crime downtown was as bad as anywhere else, and it was certainly stranger here, what with rubbery cars knocking holes in fourth-floor buildings and crawling down walls.

He thought about that. *That really was different.*

He heard sirens.

That would be the business with the hospital and the rubbery Thunderbird. They'd most likely be too busy to notice him, but it just might be best if he wasn't around, even if he would have to leave the tires and the truck.

What the hell? The truck was stolen too. He put his hands in his pockets and strolled off down the walk whistling, thinking, "Be casual, man. Be casual."

3

And, Simultaneously at Gotham Bus Terminal, Bowery Division

The bus puked diesel fumes as Batman, carrying a large paper bag, led Mandy out of the terminal with her baby against her shoulder. The little girl had awakened only once, and only for a short time, thanks to Mandy breast-feeding her.

The few people in the terminal, mostly bums and winos using the seats for a safer, slightly more comfortable place to sleep the night away, watched the big man in the bat suit and cloak with a mixture of disinterest and disbelief.

One bum, dressed in a heavy overcoat as if it were the dead of winter, watched them go out the door and onto the curb. He leaned over to the bum sleeping in the chair next to him, said, as if the guy could hear, ''It Halloween or what?''

The bum who had spoken listened a moment for an

answer. When none was forthcoming, he closed his eyes and leaned back and dozed immediately, his mouth open. A fly circled his mouth and landed on his bottom lip, crawled inside, over some stained teeth, then crawled out as if stunned, and flew off.

Outside, Batman gave Mandy a bus ticket. "I could set up an air flight."

"No," Mandy said. "I want time to think. This is great. Really."

"I hope you get your life back."

"I'll try. . . . Thanks for everything . . . the talk. The food, diapers . . ." She smiled, laughed softly.

"What?" Batman said.

"I was just thinking, you taking me into that all-night convenience store, buying the diapers and stuff. You, Batman, carrying Kerrie while I picked stuff out . . . People looking at you the way they did."

He smiled, reached out a gloved hand, and gently touched the sleeping baby on Mandy's shoulder. "Take care."

"Let's roll." It was the bus driver. He stood on the curb next to his bus, the door open at his back. He began calling out destinations. Mandy's was among them.

"This is it, then," Mandy said, and she turned to tell Batman good-bye.

He was gone. It was as if he had dissolved into the night. The diapers and the food were by her feet in the bag. She squatted carefully, so as not to disturb the baby, scooped up the bag with her free arm, looked about again.

Still no sign of him. She watched the alleyway where he had parked his car.

An instant later, the Batmobile, black and sleek with

tinted glass, pulled out of the alley next to the terminal and rolled onto the street and hummed away. Mandy said softly to its taillights, "Thanks."

She got on the bus.

Rolling through the Bowery like a low-flying missile, the Batmobile cruised. Down back streets and front streets, past shabby buildings and the stink of backed-up sewers and overturned rat- and roach-infested garbage; past dogs and cats so thin their ribs showed through their sides like venetian blinds; past old women with faces the color of soot, pushing shopping carts stuffed with other people's discards, talking to themselves; past stumbling old men with vomit-stained shirts; past tenements where the jobless lived on government checks and husbands punched out wives for entertainment; past hookers standing in shadows dark as their hopes.

Rolling over into Manchester, a working-class neighborhood with gang-ruled subdivisions—gangs by the names of the Ravens, the Turks, the Desperos, the Raging Bulls, and the Brownshirts, gangs so mean and organized they made the Leather Boys look like Boy Scouts.

On past the Van Dyke Gallery, the Gotham Racetrack, and the Manchester Viaduct. Moving on into Coventry Gardens.

Then, high up and stuck to the night, the signal: a bat confined in amber light, shining strong and bright, all the way from deep midtown.

. . . turning west now, toward the source of the light.

4

Manowack Reservation, 4:00 A.M.

The Thunderbird zoomed past the Barrett Cadillac billboard and around the curve. It turned off the main stretch and onto a red dirt road that twisted up to the used car lot and the Pyramid of Cars.

It entered the parking lot full throttle, made savage turns and spins in the center of the lot, accelerated and whirled amid rusted cars and around the dozer used for pushing them into line, about the car crusher and finally the pyramid itself, tempting fate as it did, coming perilously close to the cliff's drop-off on the pyramid's far side, so close the Barrett billboard seemed a target the Thunderbird might dive for.

Round and round, then behind the dozer again and finally the car crusher. Only this time, the Thunderbird did not reappear. A naked man staggered out from behind the crusher. He fell on his hands and knees and vomited. The vomit pooled on the ground and caught the moonlight and glowed as if filled with highly polished metal flakes. . . .

A few minutes later, the naked man climbed atop the Pyramid of Cars. At its pinnacle he had fastened an old bucket seat on a swivel. The seat's leather was ripped and gone black as rotted pecans; the swivel squeaked for need of oil. He pulled himself into the seat and relaxed. It was a perfect perch.

With a push of his foot he turned to face the billboard below, the highway beyond it. Across from the billboard, parked off the highway, he saw an old pickup. He observed it clinically. It looked as if it should be in the saddle of the car crusher, ready to be squared. Thing probably died in midmotion and had been deserted by the owner. It stayed there long enough, he might try to haul it over and make an offering of it to the crusher.

Another push of his foot and the chair spun and squeaked and he saw the mountains rising up to the night clouds, punching through them like a baker's fingers through light-crust dough. The half-moon was a gravy bowl falling out of the sky, disappearing into the gradual pink of the coming day.

A push of the foot. A squeak.

To the right of the mountains was the shack he had grown up in, dilapidated now. Shadows dangled like black spider webs over the boarded-up door and window frames. It taunted him with bad memories. It seemed at any moment his old man would come out of there with his belt in hand, ready to beat either him or his brother or their mother. Yeah, the old man, he could envision him perfectly. Angry from the whiskey and the dark color of his skin, wanting to be white and rich and at the wheel of a Thunderbird.

Well, in a way, he had gotten his wish. Behind the shack was the spot where Billy Hands, now as much Thunderbird as man, was buried, a hubcap for his marker.

He swung the chair to his left and looked at the car crusher. Until recently, it had been abandoned, like the lot. He had done a bit of mechanic work on it a short time back, had used the wench to pull an old Chevy into the saddle so he could mash it into a rusty square, and had followed it with half a dozen junkers so pitted with corrosion their automotive identity was questionable.

He had made an additional change by designing a portable switch he could work the way you worked a TV remote. He kept it in a weatherproof container attached to the bottom of the swivel seat. No more pulling levers. He merely had to set the cars in line with the wench below, then he could sit up here and push buttons and see the machine work. It was a glorious view, and the crusher did its job now as well as it had so many years ago.

He wondered if when he had used the crusher the sound of it had been heard way out on the reservation, and if those who heard it might think his father was out from beneath his hubcap, out of his block of Thunderbird, and back on the job.

But no, the mountains and the trees obstructed the car crusher noise. Most likely, it could only be heard down on the highway if you were driving slow with a window open. It was as if the hell of all automobiles was up here. The car crusher a kind of mechanical Satan, smashing the metallic souls of the less fortunate.

To his ears, the sound of it crunching the metal again

after all these years was like a lullaby—a lullaby because he had learned properly how to hate this place and all it stood for, how to turn that hate into irony. How to gain revenge for himself and the Manowacks, though the Manowacks did not know he was their avenger. They were too lost to know or understand.

The way of vengeance had been before him all the time, but he hadn't realized it until one afternoon he observed a '65 Ford Mustang drive by. He admired the Mustang, as he always admired them. Then it occurred to him that it was named after a wild horse. This was obvious, but for the first time he truly began to consider it, saw a solid connection between the machine and the animal.

The animals of olden days were the prime examples of power, speed, strength. They were the magical representatives of their time; totems and spirits were viewed in their images. But the white man had destroyed their powers and had replaced them with engines named after them, engines that ran faster and stronger than their namesakes and were worshiped and respected more mightily than any animal ever had been.

And if, as the Manowacks believed, all things animate and inanimate were alive, had what some tribes called a manitou, a magic spirit, then it stood to reason that the otherworld, the domain of the old gods, would claim the newer Mustangs and Thunderbirds and Impalas as their earthly representatives, not mangy coyotes and wolves, owls and hawks eating dead meat off the highways. And as the animals were less in sight and mind, their contours and actions would be less and less remembered in detail, unlike the automobile which was on every corner, every street, in every drive, in every garage.

Automobiles. Sleek in design, pleasant with the aroma of fresh upholstery, great windshield eyes with which their drivers, the brains of the beasts, could see out at the world. Motors they could feel between their legs and beneath their feet, the throbbing energy of potent technohorses tugging at the bit, ready to leap at the brain's command. Totems that could serve a purpose no natural totem could. They could be owned, and they could simultaneously own their "owners."

His grandfather hadn't lost his medicine, and he hadn't lost his. The totems had lost theirs. And the things he had loved as a child, and later rejected—cars—were their replacements.

He smiled as he considered this, but as the sun crawled upward, tugging down the night with its pink claws, he lost the thought and made no effort to regain it. Instead, he fastened his attention to the far side of the lot, beyond the car crusher and the rows of lost automotive souls. There he could see the clay road that wound up to the pyramid. The rising sun had given it a rusty red tint that reminded him of an old, positive battery cable. Somehow, that identification made him ill.

He turned away from the view, closed his eyes, dozed for a while. When the sun rose completely and the whole of his body was blushed red by it, he awoke, climbed down, and put on his clothes.

Clutch and Shift to—

—Third Gear

1

Bruce Wayne/Batman's Journal, Recorded 7:00 A.M.

Alfred, the strangeness I mentioned. The forthcoming storm I predicted. It's no longer forthcoming. I am in its midst.

Tonight was not much in the action department. The usual stuff. There was one nice thing: a young woman with a baby in the Bowery. I may actually have done some real good there. She had hit bottom, Alfred, and I threw her a rope. No use going into the details, but she is on a bus back to Nebraska now, and I am hopeful she will get back the life she lost. It is something to feel good about.

But the night was not really eventful in the usual sense of the word.

Until late morning and Commissioner Gordon flipped on the signal—my invitation to go midtown.

I parked in a back alley, activated the locks and alarms

on the Batmobile and took to the rooftops with my ropes and hooks. When I came over the edge of the building and behind the signal light where Jim was standing, looking out at the city, he jumped.

He always jumps.

"Dammit," he said, "don't do that. Haven't I told you not to do that? I dropped my cigar."

"It was impossible to resist," I said.

"Glad you enjoyed it." He recovered his cigar, brushed off the wet end, stuck it in his mouth, clasped his hands behind his back, and returned his attention to the city and the neon blisters throbbing in the darkness.

He glanced at me out of the corner of his eye, removed his cigar, held it between his fingers. He nodded at the view. "Pretty, isn't it?"

I lifted my chin toward the signal, said, "You light up the sky so we could discuss the view?"

"Yeah, and I thought maybe we'd have tea out here too, some little cakes to go with it. . . . Some Leather Boys were found broken up and beaten up over in the Bowery. None dead, but pretty scared. Officer came across them said they were glad to see him, told him you went crazy and jumped them. I know better than that, sure you had a reason, but you were kind of rough, weren't you?"

"I certainly hope so."

"You got to know that no matter what they did—and I'm sure they did something—there's a line even you don't step over. I just wanted to remind you of it."

I didn't say anything to that.

"Come on," he said. "Let's go to the office."

We went. It was dark in there and he didn't turn on the overhead light. There was only the moonlight and the city lights pumping rays through the venetian blinds.

He plopped down in the chair behind his desk. There was a gooseneck lamp on the corner of the desk, and he turned it on. It was a dim light. The sort you had to have right over what you're reading, and if you weren't reading, it was just a pleasant glow in the darkness, like a kid's night-light.

I sat down in the chair across from him and waited. Jim took hold of the gooseneck and twisted it so it was pooling light on my side, then he slid a file folder across to me, sat back, and waited.

He looked shrunken up inside his stained gray suit, like a cicada not wishing to come out of its husk. His white mustache was slightly tinted with tobacco, which meant he was smoking a lot more than usual, and that meant he was more nervous than usual. He had cut back on the cigars and the pipe a lot in the last few years, but when things got tense, out they came. He uses them the way a bored dog does a chew toy.

He was nervous because he had chosen to call me in. City Hall loves that. They want it to look like any crime solved in Gotham is solved by them, without outside interference.

I know it is old news to you, Alfred, but I can never forget that when I first appeared on the scene they treated me like a vigilante, and perhaps they were right. But I'm a "legal vigilante" now. Sanctioned, if not enjoyed, by the department. They decided they might as well make me legal, since I was going to do what I did anyway, with or without their blessings. And, of course, by symbolically giving me a badge, anything I accomplish they can claim part of the glory. But it is such sour glory, I cannot altogether blame their feelings toward me.

In all fairness to the department, I do something in the city, solve a crime, wreck a racket, you can bet, dressed the way I dress, that I am going to get some press. But the everyday man in blue, out there beating the street, the hard-working detectives who go at it without glamour, if they solve something, it ends up on the back page of the *Gotham Times*, behind the entertainment section. Makes it look as if they do nothing and I do everything.

I opened the folder, pushed it beneath the light. The file was on the hit-and-run of a few nights back. The one I had been peripherally involved with. Instead of laying it all out here, let me capsulize the contents. If doubts should arise as to my recall, or if your interest goes beyond my generalization of the events, the complete file is available. Also available are my cross-hatching and research notes, conducted via computer bank. You know the codes.

There were photos.

FIRST PHOTO:

Narrow dead-end alley. Shot taken from the entrance.

SECOND PHOTO:

Alley from the rear wall looking toward the street. Across the street the plate glass window of Gotham Boot and Leather is visible. A fire hydrant.

THIRD PHOTO:

A man. Lying on the ground. Bad shape. A leg gone. Blood all around. Belt tourniquet on his mauled leg, high above where the knee used to be. Looks to be in his thirties.

On the back of the photo was written: *Harders McCammon. Dead on the scene.*

FOURTH PHOTO:

A body, twisted into the garbage of the alley by spinning tires. Its sex not identifiable. A mess. A large ugly stain visible on the alley wall near the body.

On the back was: *Victim later identified as Marilyn Jane Cass. Age 34.*

FIFTH PHOTO:

One mug shot of the kid, Bill Thomas, split down the middle to display front and profile views.

REMAINING PHOTOS:

Various angles on the alley and the bodies.

There were statements also. They include those by the arresting officer, Sergeant O'Herity, and the kid I grabbed, one Bill Thomas. They reveal little more than the fact that a hit-and-run took place in the alley and that the kid robbed the bodies of not only money, but in the case of Harders McCammon, his shoes and leg as well.

Thomas claimed to have seen the car that killed the pair coming out of the alley nose first, a black classic Thunderbird.

The general report concluded from the evidence and the condition of the bodies that the victims had been mauled by a spinning automobile, but it was also noted that the logic of the evidence was contrary to the logic of available space, the alley being only wide enough to *possibly* accommodate a single automobile, and that automobile, once reaching the dead end, would be forced to back out, as no turnaround space was available. Or, if Thomas can be believed, indications are the car went in backwards and came out forwards, but this would not explain the evidence of spinning.

Next page had a report by the senior lab technician, Ms. Mavis Gould. It read:

> It's unfortunate, but somehow the rubber residue taken from the skid marks in the alley and the connecting street, as well as the black paint found embedded in the skin of the deceased, Marilyn Jane Cass, and on the amputated leg of the deceased, Harders McCammon, seems to have been lost, or confused with the results of another test.
>
> What we have labeled as rubber residue is actually human skin. The evidence labeled as car paint is also human skin, as well as hair, blood, and saliva.
>
> I'm confused as to how this mistake could have occurred, as I oversaw the examination of these items myself, and the strictest procedure was followed.

I closed the file and looked up. "They lost the evidence?"

"They're looking the lab over for it, trying to figure how things got misfiled. But Mavis, the lady who wrote the report, she was in here today, says she thinks things weren't misfiled, that the results are correct."

He paused to suck in some cigar smoke.

"She said the materials they examined looked like rubber and paint, but it wasn't rubber and paint when subjected to chemical analysis. They tried doing the job again, using the leftover evidence, and the material had changed outright to flesh and blood. On the report she says it was some kind of mistake because it seemed like the only logical thing to say, formal report like that, but when I talked to her in private, she was upset and sang a different tune. Said she was certain the evidence had altered."

"What do you think?"

"She's the best lab technician this department's seen. And though I'm not entirely ready to believe the stuff actually changed, I believe she believes it.

"But there's yet another in a long line of kickers. The flesh and blood when examined as flesh and blood didn't belong to the victims."

"I assume there's more?"

"I'll say. This hit-and-run got me thinking about one a week ago in Glendale. Hit-and-runs happen all the time. Accidents mostly. Someone driving too fast and a pedestrian steps out in front of them, and—bam! Driver hits them, panics, drives off.

"Nine times out of ten, you hear from them not long after. Next day. A week or so later. Guilty conscience. But this guy, salesman name of Heilman, he was killed in his living room. A car slammed through the wall while he was watching the boob tube, left out of there with him lying on the floor with a head the size of a roof shingle, a picture tube and a couch spring in his chest. Guy and the place were so messed up, couldn't tell what was him and what was the furniture."

"Not a pretty image."

"Yeah. And you know how the sheriff's department is over there, with Sheriff Carruthers not ready to accept that his office is ultimately under the jurisdiction of Gotham City—my jurisdiction—"

"I know," I said.

"—but they're the law too, and if they wanted to call the case their own, I was ready to let them. Figured they could do what I could do on something like that, and the sweeter we could keep relations, the better. I get enough headaches from Carruthers without adding one more. But I did force them to give me a look at their report."

The flame had gone out on Jim's cigar, and he paused to relight it. He puffed on the vile thing, blew out smoke, watched it spiral in the dim light, glide into darkness. "When I asked for the file, they started shuffling. Carruthers said it wasn't that he wouldn't show it to me, but he didn't have it to show. Said he was deeply embarrassed, but they had lost the evidence. All they knew for sure was that the victim was murdered and it was no accident.

"As for the loss of the file, I hated that, of course, but I've got to admit, there was a part of me that liked watching that know-it-all Carruthers squirm like a worm on a hot griddle. Still, bottom line is, I had to mark the loss of the file up to fate, give Carruthers and his staff a reprimand, hope the evidence, or new evidence, turned up."

"But you're thinking now they didn't lose the file?"

"Shall we play Holmes and Watson?"

"All right," I said. "You think Carruthers lied to you. That they ran their tests and came up with the same thing your staff came up with. Carruthers didn't want to tell you he lost the file, but he preferred that to letting you know his staff was incompetent and got the evidence confused, that they came up with blood and skin instead of rubber and paint. He lost a little face that way, but thought the other way, showing such peculiar results, would make him look even worse. How am I doing?"

"You're batting a thousand, as usual. . . . 'Course, I could be wrong. They could have actually lost the file, but for my taste, it's too big a coincidence to dismiss. There's more, but I'll tell you the rest while you drive us over to Gotham Memorial."

"All right, but light one cigar in my car, and I break your arm."

Jim gathered up a set of the files for me, and a tape recorder. I didn't ask about the recorder. We went downstairs and walked around to where I had parked the car.

Jim put the files and the recorder on the seat between us. When I pulled away from the curb he said, "Drive slow. I want to get all this out before we get there. Other day there was a double hit-and-run in Cold Shepherd. Doctor there used to work in our coroner's office. Little trouble with the booze. You know her—"

"Catherine Meadows. Good woman. Real pro."

"That's the one. Serves as both doctor and coroner over there. She sent in some evidence for our lab to evaluate. Evidence from a hit-and-run. Would you like to venture a guess?"

"Results were the same as the evidence on the Webb Street hit-and-run."

"Yeah, and this time Mavis said she was standing by the results, no matter how weird, and if anyone wanted to think she was incompetent, so be it. She was taking any and all blame for the results, exonerating her staff of any mishandling. She offered me her resignation if I wanted it. I didn't, of course. I'm still reluctant to believe the test results are correct, but two out of two makes one ponder, doesn't it? What was it Sherlock Holmes said about things like this? Something about how if you ruled out the possible, then you were left to believe the impossible?''

''Close enough,'' I said.

Jim was quiet for a time, mentally organizing his thoughts. I took a few unnecessary turns to stretch the trip out. When he started up again, his words came slow and careful.

''Final note of weirdness came over an hour ago, but before I tell you about it, I need to tell you that one of the hit-and-run victims in Cold Shepherd lived. Guy named Evan Hill. He was bad off, lost both legs, semi-comatose. Kept muttering about a Thunderbird. Yesterday, Catherine Meadows called and told me about what happened there, and that she needed some help from the department here. Also told me she was having Hill transferred to Memorial. Felt a big hospital could do more for him.

''Well, I was at the office working late, or working early, depending on how you look at it, when I got a call that there was trouble at the hospital. When I heard about it, I went over there and took a look, put what I saw together with the crimes I told you about, and decided to bring you in. It's your kind of case.''

Jim picked up the recorder. ''This will take care of the rest of it for you. Taped here are recorded statements from the nurse, janitor, and a security guard over at Memorial. Listen.''

Alfred, let me pause to say that the statements of the nurse, janitor, and guard were given to me on cassette, and I have transferred them to our system, along with my introductions. It's available to you on the audio portion of the computer. Press AUDIO.

[illegible]

[illegible]

2

Audio Computer:

VOICE OF BRUCE WAYNE: The report of Jane Modell, the night duty nurse, follows:

> I was sitting at the desk, not really thinking about much of anything. It had been a slow night, you see, and all of a sudden I felt a kind of chill. Not like the air conditioner gives. The kind you get when you're being watched. I looked up, and from here, as you can see, anyone coming in the emergency room entrance, or making an exit out of it, is visible. Well, a man was standing there and the door was closing behind him and he was looking at me. That wasn't so odd, but he was buck naked. Now, I'll tell you, I'm not bashful. I mean, I *am* a nurse, but that's different. Not that the guy was any bad thing to look at, you

know. He looked all right without his clothes. Athletic, in his thirties, dark, handsome, American Indian–looking, maybe Italian. I don't know.

He didn't seem self-conscious about being naked, I can assure you of that. Just stood there looking, like he could see through me.

He didn't appear to be hurt or dazed, anything like that, but my first impression was he'd had his clothes torn off of him in a fight, a wreck, something like that, and had wandered in here looking for help. I spoke softly to him, calm like, said, "Sir, you okay?" He didn't answer. He walked over here and took the roster book from in front of me, and since I'm not supposed to let anyone see it without the right permissions, I tried to stop him, tried to reason with him. I began to think he was a mental patient, or maybe someone who had lost his memory and had already been admitted to the hospital but had gotten out of bed.

Really, I don't know what I thought. He had hold of that roster book at one end, and I got hold of it at the other. We played tug-of-war for a moment, then he reached over the desk and palmed me in the face and shoved me against the wall.

I didn't go down, but when I came off the wall and was going to start for him, well, I don't know. I looked at his eyes and . . . looking into them was like the feeling you get when you're up somewhere high and you look over the edge, and for some reason you get the urge to jump. . . .

Know what I'm saying? I was scared, I won't lie to you, and I don't scare easily. I'm a big lady, and I've wrestled with a few nuts and druggies in my time. You work here long enough at the night desk, it's going to happen, but this guy, uh-uh, I didn't want any part of him. Had I grabbed for that book again, it would have been like leaning too far over that high place, you know?

Guy finished looking at the roster, tossed it on the desk, and walked to the elevator.

I waited a second, then went from behind the desk, peeped around the corner, and watched his bare tush rolling along. He went into the elevator and closed the doors. I pushed the button that calls security, got on the phone, and dialed nine-one-one.

VOICE OF BRUCE WAYNE: Jim Franklin, fourth floor janitor:

Well, I was in the mop closet down at the far end of the hall, see. Had the door open and was standing there at the floor sink with the water running on a mop, getting ready to wring it out and do a little damp moppin', 'cause I'd waxed it the night before and that was all it needed to give it a shine. There's some people will wax a floor to death, get it all built up so it'll turn kinda yellow on you, but not me, I'm a pro.

But see, I'm about to mop the floor, and I hear the elevator door pinging like it'll do, and I turned to look, and this fella steps out of there and he don't have no clothes on. Not a stitch. Well, I stared at him, and he turned and stared at me, and the way he did made me feel like I was the one naked. I started wishing that mop closet door was closed and locked. He kind of smiled, you know, like we was pals or something, and you can bet I did me some big smiling back. Then he looked across the hall at a door, getting the number, and started walking the other way, checking the numbers as he went.

While he was doing that, I got out of the closet, after wringing my mop out, 'cause you leave one wet, you come back after too long it gets a stink on it you can't hardly kill, and then I cruised on down the stairs, 'cause the elevator was too close to where he was. When I got to the first floor Miss Modell was already on the horn calling everybody in the world.

I went into the supply room and got me a bed rail to conk that fella with, 'cause even though he hadn't done nothing to me, Miss Modell told me he'd pushed her down, and I got to tell you, if ever I looked at someone and thought, now there's a fella needs some conkin', he was it. From upstairs there come all kinds of racket, even a horn honking—like a car horn—and it was beeping that ole shave and a haircut thing, like the best time in the world was goin' on up there, then there was that big explosion, or ramming was more like it, and things got quiet as grandma's grave.

He didn't never come down, so I didn't get to try and conk him. Next thing I know, the law's running upstairs, looking around and coming down with nothing, and saying how the wall was knocked through to the outside and asking questions and all. It was my break about then, so when they got through with me, I went and had me a sandwich and a strawberry pop, and I don't guess I got nothing else I can say about it all.

VOICE OF BRUCE WAYNE: Bill Silverman, the night security man:

It was my break time, I want to make that clear, and I was sitting on the wall around the flower beds drinking coffee on the opposite side of the building. So I get this beep on my pager, and the way it's set up, you can tell by the way it beeps who's calling, so I started walking around the building on my way to the night nurse's station.

Before I could get around the building there was a noise, like an explosion, and I hit the ground, case someone was firing at me. I was in Korea, and I still get the willies when a loud noise happens, like a car backfires or something heavy is dropped.

Anyway, time I got up and round there, wasn't nothing to see but this black Thunderbird speeding off the lot, and it was a beauty, but kind of different too, like it was a special-made rig or something. It was really moving, and looking back now, I suppose it had something to do with what happened, but I don't know what. Time I got around there and was talking to Jane, I guess it was already over, though she and the janitor thought the guy was still upstairs.

I pulled my gun and went up the stairs and looked around and saw the door to the room on the end was open, and I went in and took a look. . . . Saw the mess and the hole in the wall, but wasn't any naked man around. I got a little sick from the way it smelled in there, the blood and all, so I went down and had a cup of coffee and waited for the police to come.

VOICE OF BRUCE WAYNE: End of audio portion of computer journal. Press J and RETURN.

3

Bruce Wayne/Batman's Journal Continued

By the time the tape was finished, we had arrived at the Gotham Memorial parking lot. The wall facing us, four stories up, had a huge gap in it and light was shining out of the gap and there was a group of blue suits standing around in the lot and over by the side entrance.

Inside, we passed the admittance desk. There was a male nurse behind it. He looked a little excited, or perhaps disappointed because he had missed all the action. I assumed Miss Modell had gone home.

We rode the elevator to the fourth floor. When we stepped into the hallway there was the smell of death in the air, blood and feces, mixed with the usual smells of a hospital, as well as a couple of smells I didn't immediately recognize, primarily because they were out of place.

We walked to the last door on the left. A blue suit was standing there. He stepped aside.

Before we entered, Jim tapped a finger on the name card outside the door. It read: EVAN HILL.

Inside were a number of technicians. They were moving cautiously about because the floor looked ready to give way in numerous locations. One pale-faced blue suit stood silently nearby, obviously trying to wish himself away.

On the far side of the room, where a set of windows had formerly been positioned in the wall, was a gaping hole that looked as if it had been knocked there by a tank. Starlight came through the breach. For a moment it seemed as if a less benign universe was collapsing into this one, filling it up.

The overhead lights had been shaken down by whatever had happened in the room, so the forensic boys had brought in a few flood lights, and in their glow I could see the mess that had once been a bed with Evan Hill on it. Now it was a tangle of reddened sheets and human flesh twisted into the metal frame of the hospital bed. It appeared as if someone had run the bed and its contents through an immense blender, then hammered the mess flat, driving much of it into the floor. Spotted all over the floor were what looked like tight black doughnuts. Automotive rubber burns.

That, of course, didn't make sense, as there was barely enough room for a motorcycle to cut doughnuts in the room, and yet the size of the marks belied what was reasonable.

Other than the technicians and the blue suit and the general condition of the room, I noticed the smells, the ones I mentioned before, and now I was able to sort them out. Tire rubber, of course, and the faintest whiff of carbon monoxide.

Jim said, "In spite of the way it looks, there's no real indication of a bomb. Wall was probably knocked out, not exploded. And you see that the body looks to have been more mashed than blown up."

"And you haven't a clue where the naked man went?"

"Not unless he's mashed up in this mess, and I doubt that. But if he isn't, and he's responsible for this, where did he go? We've searched the hospital top to bottom, and no dice.

"Apparently he went out the hole in the wall there, but to do that, he'd have to have been a fly, or you. If he jumped, well, it's some kind of drop, and we'd have found him out there on the ground, making like a bearskin rug. And those rubber burns on the floor, want to bet what shows up when they're analyzed?"

"No," I said, "but I would like samples."

"Done." Jim went over to the technicians and told them what I needed. I walked around the room and tried to pick up on a clue. There were too many of them, and none of them made sense. I went over to the gap in the wall and stood there and looked out at the parking lot. I pulled my pocket flash and got down on my stomach and leaned out the gap and turned the beam on the outside wall, saw that there were rubber burns going down it, like huge snail trails.

I got up and called Jim over. "Tell your people to get samples of the rubber on the outside wall."

"What?"

I pointed and gave him the flashlight. He got down on

his stomach and took a look. "I'll be damned," he said. He stood and gave me my light. "You know, until I came here to Gotham, met you, I dealt with ordinary crime. Murder, rape, burglary, that sort of thing. But when you showed up, a whole new kind of crime showed up. Know what I'm saying?"

"I should have been an accountant?"

"That comes to mind," he said. "It's like this stuff has to exist so someone like you can deal with it."

"So if I retire things will return to normal?"

"Hey, I'm talking. Truth is, it's gotten so I look at you and you don't seem stupid in that outfit. I don't know what's normal anymore. You could cut down on the size of those ears, though, they seem a little much."

"I'll tell my tailor."

"You do that."

The blue suit called to Jim. He went over and came back with a packet of samples one of the technicians had prepared for me. I put it in the pouch inside my cape.

The blue suit called Jim back for something, and I pulled a hook and line from my utility belt and fastened the hook to the edge of the hole in the wall. I swung out and down, hung by one hand, used the other to shine my little flash against the wall. Definitely rubber burns.

I heard Jim talking above me. "Now where in hell did he go? I hate it when he does that."

I put the light away, slid down the line to the sidewalk, popped the hook free and let it rewind into my belt's retracting device, and began walking to the Batmobile. I wanted to be alone, to think. Jim could get a ride home with one of his men.

Jim called out to me. "I see you this time, dammit. I see you. You're no ghost."

I looked back and up at him. He was standing in the gap, floodlights framing him from behind. I waved at him, went to the Batmobile, and drove away from there, rushing to get home before daybreak.

4

Wayne Manor, 9:22 A.M.

Bruce saw lights and the lights were very bright and very round. They hung in a dusky sky and were neither suns nor moons but were rimmed with silver, and there was a shape behind them and the shape was long and sleek and shadowy.

He felt himself being pulled back, as if on a camera dolly, and he could see the lights hanging evenly in the sky, maybe eight feet apart (or perhaps it was eighty feet apart, distance was impossible to judge—like a child staring at the moon and seeing it the size of a nickel and only a little higher than a house, while an adult sees it as miles away, beyond the atmosphere of the earth), and he could identify more of the shadowy shape behind the lights, and the shape became less shadowy with a wink of grillwork that hung beneath the two great lights, and the grillwork twisted like teeth grinding gristle. The grillwork split wide, revealing a deep, dark mouth where a tongue the color of terminal cancer and freshly poured asphalt flexed and flicked.

Then, as if lying on his back on a grease rack and the grease rack rising, Bruce could see up and above the lights, and there was something else up there. A dark windshield, catching rays from the headlights, making them flicker like fireflies before releasing them to be consumed by the surrounding darkness, brilliant treats for the ravenous belly of doom.

What he was looking at was an enormous car. It dangled in the sky at a slightly downward angle, the headlights giving glow to what was below.

As the rising grease rack position afforded him greater view of the heavens, he saw that towering above the colossal automobile he had identified was the sloping roof of one even greater, and way, way up at the top of the greater car he could make out a stupendous sunroof, and though there was no sun shining through it, there were lights, and they were like a heaven full of stars, or maybe a multitude of smaller, headlighted cars roving about the galaxy of this automotive night; a night beyond which lived the gods of clean carburetors, fresh upholstery smells, and smooth gearshifts.

Now the grease rack view was gone. Bruce's vision was lowering. He was upright, walking down an alley. Beside him, on the right, was his mother, fashionably dressed, blond and pretty, a string of pearls about her neck. On the left was his father, tall, handsome, muscular, in an expensive suit and overcoat. Behind them were marquee lights, and between the rectangle of lights, in black letters on a white background was THE MARK OF ZORRO, and below that was a flash of poster showing Zorro with wheels below his knees instead of shins, ankles, and feet. The sword in his hand was an overlong oil stick.

Looking left, beyond his father, Bruce saw that the sides of the alley were tinted car windshields, and below them were rows of door handles set into black upholstery. To the right, the same. At his feet was a floorboard carpet filled with dust and wads of chewing gum.

When he looked up, he saw that his parents had changed. His mother, like Zorro, was now rolling along on wheels. Her eyes were small headlights. The pearls at her neck were polished ball bearings.

His father was on wide truck wheels; his eyes were headlights on high beam. As he rolled along he smiled at Bruce, and in place of teeth his mouth was filled with grillwork, like a classic Buick.

Bruce discovered he too was on wheels. He was a brightly painted kiddie car. His eyes lit up his path.

A wheeled man, his headlights flickering nervously from high to low, pulled out of the darkness and into their path. He pointed an arm forward. There wasn't a hand at the end of it; it was tipped with a greasy black pistol.

ABRUPT FLASH TO FILM STRUCTURE:

INSERT: CLOSE ON PISTOL:

Side of the pistol, and it's made up of little black wheels, turning, turning . . .

CLOSER YET:

Wheels are small humans, naked, bent double, feet in their mouths, bodies covered in smoking lube oil and axle grease. Tiny muffled voices attempt to sound out around foot-filled mouths. Results: noises as weak and sad as worn-out ignition switches.

BACK TO SCENE:

As Bruce, Mother, and Father cease rolling (brakes snap hard enough to give whiplash) and Mother recoils in horror. Father guns his motor and rolls in front of Bruce and Mother, protectively spreads his arms, and—

CUT TO MAN WITH GUN:

Beads of oil on his forehead. The gun rides up and spits—

SLOW MO AND CLOSE ON:

—little silver race car exiting the pistol barrel, cruising through the air, miniature tires—minuscule humans with their feet in their mouths—spinning on an invisible highway, car's silvery color capturing the overhead beams, holding them until it enters Father's chest and tugs the reflections, like a JUST MARRIED car pulling bright confetti, after it.

PULL BACK, FULL VIEW OF:

Father going down, oil flying out of his mouth, mixing with the dust and gum on the floorboard.

BACK TO AND CLOSE ON:

—Gun in the man's hand as it jumps again. Another race car shoots out of the barrel.

MOVING WITH THE BULLET/CAR AS:

—It strikes Mother's chest, shattering her necklace. The ball bearings fly away like a planetary system minus gravity.

QUICK CUT TO AND CLOSE ON A BALL BEARING SPINNING ON THE FLOORBOARD, TWIRLING LIGHT LIKE A DANCER WITH FIRE BATONS:

QUICK CUT TO:

BRUCE'S VIEW, WHICH HAS ALTERED SO THAT

NOW IT'S AS IF HE'S SEATED IN THE CAR THAT HANGS OVER THE SCENE:

He sees the gunman/car panicking, spinning on his tires, shifting internal gears, floorboarding away, followed by a cloud of burned rubber and carbon-black exhaust. He sees himself, the little car, standing over his fallen parents, rocking wildly on his wheels, watching their lube oil, transmission fluid, radiator water, and antifreeze pool around them. He screams a noise not unlike the sound of an ill-adjusted fan belt squeaking.

No mechanic on duty.

SCENE SPINS AND:

the film motif is lost and the car from which Bruce observes all this begins to gyrate, like an enormous tire centered on a coal-colored hub, faster and faster, and then it soars up high with a wail, sprouts enormous batwings.

And now Bruce is the bat, and from this position (bats-eye view) he can see clearly again, and what he sees below is the earth, and it's the shape of a small tire, turning slowly, to no purpose, to no gain. . . .

5

Bruce awoke from the dream, shattered.

He sat up in bed and there was Alfred beside him, a hand on his shoulder. In spite of that, he felt as if he had merely awakened from a dream within a dream. The hand felt solid enough, but was it? How solid was solid in a dream within a dream?

"I heard you scream," Alfred said. "A weak scream, sir. It frightened me more than usual. It sounded like a squeaky wheel. I thought perhaps you were having a heart attack."

"Depends on what sort of heart attack you mean, Alfred."

"Of course, sir."

"Alfred?"

"Yes, sir?"

"The dream was different this time."

"It often varies."

"I mean very different. It had a film motif as it often has—"

"Due to the fact your parents were killed after a movie."

"Right, but there was also a car motif."

"Nothing odd about that, sir. You are currently quite involved with automotive concerns. You're aware, of course, I've been reading your journal and case reports?"

"My subconscious is trying to tell me something, Alfred."

"Meaning that you've found some truths your conscious mind is not yet ready to accept?"

"That's right. . . . This dream was so real."

"Those are the good ones, sir."

"Nothing good about it."

"Not exactly how I meant it, Master Bruce."

"I know. . . . Alfred, how real is a dream? Tell me."

"I suppose as real as you allow it to be, Master Bruce. Are we into the 'is life but a dream within a dream' mode, sir?"

"I suppose we are."

"Been reading your Sartre, Kierkegaard, Camus again, I see. They always set you in a black and introspective mood. Well, sir, if we are a dream—and for sake of argument, let us say that the dream is an unhappy one—then could we not alter our dreams in the same way we alter our lives? Make them more pleasant? I believe I could do that, provided I thought I was a dream within a dream within a dream, or whatever. I don't, however. But we've had this conversation before?"

"Too many times."

"And nothing I've said before matters, so I'm reluctant to haul out the same baggage."

"It may not seem like it, but it helps. Really."

"Personally, sir, if I were you and you were asking my advice, I would take it. It's undoubtedly the best you'll get from anyone."

"I don't doubt that, but . . ."

"You quite prefer the misery? Is that it, sir? A kind of penance? A martyr complex, perhaps?"

"That's possible."

"Probable, Master Bruce. And not to bore you with a repeated comment, but it wasn't your fault your parents were murdered. You were a little boy."

"It doesn't help, Alfred."

"A cup of hot cocoa, then?"

"Cocoa?"

"As we've been over this subject repeatedly, the choices seem somewhat limited for this kind of thing, sir. It's best to think in a basic manner. Simple-pleasures, and all that."

"I see your point, Alfred. Thanks. Hot cocoa will be fine."

"It may not be the answer to your problems, sir, but as the Southerners might say, it beats being jobbed in the nose with a broken limb."

"Jabbed in the eye with a pointed stick, Alfred."

"That as well, sir. I'll be right back with the cocoa."

"Bring it down to the cave."

Bruce swung from beneath the covers and plucked his robe off the bedpost and slipped it on.

"Very well, sir. I suppose you will be going down to do flips and jumps and perform all manner of athletic endeavor?"

"Am I so predictable?"

"To an adversary on the street, I'm sure you're quite greasy, sir—"

"Slippery, Alfred, not greasy."

"That as well. But to me, you're as reliable and predictable as the ticking of Big Ben. And, somewhat off the subject, might I add that you are quite the cutup, sir. Constantly cheery. Always full of good news. I continuously find my association with you to be one of everlasting humor. Indeed, *lighthearted* is your middle name."

Bruce finished tying his robe. "Do I detect a large dose of irony, Alfred?"

"That would quite depend on your level of perception, Master Bruce. Irony might not be entirely in tune with your consciousness, though it is certainly in tune with your nature."

"The cocoa, Alfred."

"Might I suggest less jumping off of buildings and bounding about in a Halloween costume, and more reading in the library, and perhaps Dickens instead of Sartre and those writers preoccupied with the meaning of it all? That sort of thing would give most anyone bad dreams. The answer to life is much more akin to regular bathroom habits, a good friend, a hot cup of cocoa. One doesn't live for the dead, sir. One lives for the living. Remember, dwelling on your parents' deaths denies the memory of their lives."

"I remember them, Alfred, but not well. I'm not denying their worth in life, because I don't truly remember them in life. What I remember is . . . that night, the moment I lost them. I suppose what I recall is more a mythology of who I want them to have been than who they really were. I fear I never really knew them, and I miss never finishing my childhood. I never had that opportunity."

"Nor will you, sir. That's a fact and one that cannot be altered, no matter what you do, no matter how you live your life. Therefore, one must move on. Bury the dead. Psychiatry 101, and a page torn from the All-Knowing Book of Alfred Pennyworth."

"Just get the cocoa, Alfred."

"The cocoa, sir."

Alfred moved toward the door.

"Alfred?"

Without turning: "Yes, sir."

"Thanks for listening . . . again. And you're right, of course."

"Of course, sir."

"But it doesn't help. Logic merely confuses the issue."

Alfred opened the door, stood for a moment as if collecting himself, and just before stepping out of the room said, "I know, son."

The door closed and left Bruce in darkness.

6

Alfred, carrying a tray with a cup of steaming cocoa on it, touched the tall grandfather clock with a finger and the front of it sprang open. Alfred stepped inside and the clock door closed automatically behind him.

He went down the long row of stone steps and into the well-lit cave, past trophy cases, past freestanding trophies: a giant penny, a mammoth playing card bearing the Joker's likeness, a life-sized mechanical Tyrannosaurus Rex—reminders of Batman's more unique adventures.

He considered those, thought, *Maybe Master Bruce and I both live in a dream. This is a most unusual life.* Then he thought, *Now he's got me doing it.*

He continued down.

Bruce, wearing only a pair of gray sweatpants, was swinging between the parallel bars, his body shiny with sweat, the muscles rolling beneath his skin like rubber balls in a tight nylon bag.

He swung his legs up, twisted, let go of the bars and

flipped, went high and came down between them again, his arms flashing out, his hands fastening on the bars like metal pinchers. He swung again, out and away from the bars, landed on the worn gray mat, tumbled forward, and came up on his feet.

He glided to the heavy hanging bag, jabbed it, right crossed it, left hooked and kicked it, followed with rapid blows from his knees, elbows, and forehead.

Now he was away from the bag, leaping for the hanging rings, swinging between them as if he were a part of their construction. Feet over his head, twisting completely, letting go, hitting the mat on the balls of his feet, springing up and snatching the rings again, bending, rotating, swinging.

Alfred had watched Bruce work out innumerable times before, but it never ceased to amaze him. He had never seen anyone so dedicated, so perfect. Bruce was a world-class gymnast, as well as one of the greatest martial arts experts living. No, he was undoubtedly *the* greatest martial arts expert living. Had he chosen, he could have been heavyweight boxing champion of the world, kick boxing and full-contact karate champion of the world. Of this Alfred was certain. No one had been tested as many times as Bruce had. No one had successfully battled so many opponents—one at a time, ten at a time, armed and unarmed.

Bruce was on the forty-foot climbing rope now, scurrying up it like a monkey. When he reached the top, he came down suddenly, falling two feet at a time, hands snapping out to grab the rope and save himself as he dropped, letting go again, clutching, letting go, clutching, repeating all the way down.

When he hit the matting, Bruce immediately went into the beautiful, slow-motion forms of t'ai chi. The movements of a ballet dancer couldn't have been more beautiful and precise.

Alfred walked to the computer banks, placed the tray of cocoa in front of the main terminal and turned it on, inserted and punched up Bruce's comments concerning last night. He had read them earlier, but their strangeness prompted him to read them again.

When he finished, he decided to look at the research and notes Bruce had recorded beyond his journal. As it was more technical and recapped and reevaluated already existing material, he hadn't bothered with it before. His concern was generally Bruce's disposition more than the case at hand, but this case was strange and compelling, and he felt perhaps he might ease Bruce's mind a bit by offering a helpful suggestion. He liked doing that on the tougher matters.

He tapped it onto the screen. It read:

FIRST ATTACK

VICTIM'S NAME: Jerry Heilman.

OCCUPATION: Shoe Salesman for the Greater Footwear Corporation, offices Gotham City, New York, Los Angeles, and Dallas, Texas. Type of sales involved in: traveling door-to-door salesman.

GENERAL STATS: Place of birth, New Jersey. Educated Gotham City High School, eleventh grade. Recently retired to Glendale. Bachelor. No surviving relatives. Victim of hit-and-run murder in Glendale. Age 50.

PERTINENT DATA: Murder took place in the victim's home. An automobile ran through the living room wall, struck, killed, and mutilated the body of Heilman to such an extent that couch springs, television tray, and a forty-two-inch color television set could not easily be separated from the remains of the body. Evidence of the crime: paint and tire rubber samples were presumably lost in a laboratory mix-up. Cover-up of true laboratory results expected due to possible odd nature of findings and ill feelings between Sheriff Carruthers and the Gotham Police Department. Final note: Greater Footwear Corporation is known for selling cheap footwear across the country and for concentrating especially on poverty areas such as ghettos, barrios, and Indian reservations.

SECOND ATTACK

VICTIM'S NAME: (1) Marilyn Jane Cass

OCCUPATION: Director of Gotham City Museum's Division of Antiquity.

GENERAL STATS: Place of birth, Gotham City. Educated Gotham City High School. Vassar, Ph.D. Anthropology and Archaeology. Internship, Manowack Indian Reservation. Museum position established shortly thereafter. Serious relationship with Harders, McCammon, also a victim of the attack.

PERTINENT DATA: Murdered in alley off Webb Street by hit-and-run vehicle. Body mauled beyond recognition. Paint and tire rubber samples analyzed. Results thought to be confused. On closer examination they proved to be blood and skin from an American Indian.

NOTE: Obvious similarities between this attack and the one on Jerry Heilman.

VICTIM: (2) Harders McCammon

OCCUPATION: Computer Programmer for Gotham Mutual and Life Insurance Corporation.

GENERAL STATS: Place of birth, Nacogdoches,

Texas. Educated, Nacogdoches School District. Two years Tyler Junior College, Tyler, Texas. Two years LaBorde University, LaBorde, Texas. Resident of Gotham City. Serious relationship with Marilyn Jane Cass, aforementioned (1) victim of hit-and-run attack.

INTERESTING DATA: Lost a leg in the attack. Less mauled than other victims, thought to be due to having been knocked into and partially protected by garbage and garbage cans. Survived long enough to apply a makeshift tourniquet. Thought to have been beaten with his own leg and robbed after the hit-and-run by a street tough, Bill Thomas.

NOTE: See results of laboratory data concerning previous victims.

THIRD ATTACK

VICTIM'S NAME: (1) Martha Lynn Peel

OCCUPATION: Librarian for Cold Shepherd Public Library. Age 32.

GENERAL STATS: Place of Birth, Cold Shepherd. Educated Cold Shepherd School District. Graduated bachelor's degree Library Science Gotham City University.

INTERESTING DATA: Attack similar to that of aforementioned hit-and-run victims. Body mauled beyond recognition.

VICTIM'S NAME: (2) Evan Hill.

OCCUPATION: Sometime handyman. Referred to in Cold Shepherd reports, which I computer-accessed this morning of July 30th, as the town drunk. Nothing much known about his past life. Appeared in Cold Shepherd in the sixties and remained. Possibly from the Midwest.

INTERESTING DATA: Hill was attacked same night and area as Martha Lynn Peel. Survived attack, transferred to Gotham Memorial for specialized medical attention. Murdered in his hospital bed by what appeared to be another hit-and-run attack. Evan Hill and the room he occupied were demolished and the automobile—for it seems unlikely it could have been anything else—must have exited through the hospital wall and proceeded four stories *down* the outside wall.

PERSONAL OBSERVATIONS ON HIT-AND-RUN CRIMES: Sheriff of Cold Shepherd is a Manowack Indian named Pale Boy. This gives three obvious ties to the reservation outside of Cold Shepherd: (1) Marilyn Jane Cass served her apprenticeship on the reservation; (2) Pale Boy was born and raised there; (3) Jerry Heilman sold shoes to low-income families, among them American Indians on reservations, and most certainly to members of the Manowack tribe.

Is this a clue or a coincidence?

Lastly, as a follow-up, I ran through my laboratory the blood work samples given me by Gordon, and found surface analysis to reveal the same results garnered by Gotham City's police lab.

It occurred to me that the police lab would not feel it necessary to conduct further investigation, as these results would appear too far afield of the expected. So I conducted the test further, and under computer-magnified microscopes the samples proved even more enigmatic. The blood is infected with some strange malady that resembles a virus, though I hesitate to call it such. In fact, the virus are unlike anything within my scientific experience. They're wheel-shaped. Wheels within wheels, in fact, constantly spinning, as if carrying some invisible chassis through the bloodstream. An hour later, the wheels were gone and the blood was normal.

Mysteries within mysteries.

Conclusions to follow soon.

I hope.

Alfred ceased reading and drank Bruce's cocoa. It was getting cool anyway and Bruce never ate what was prepared when Alfred prepared it. Quite frustrating, actually, cooking meals and watching them cool. It would teach the boy a lesson.

Alfred carefully examined the photos in the file. Something in one of them caught his eye. He took a small magnifying glass from the desk drawer and put it to the photograph. As he suspected. Jolly good.

Bruce strolled over, wiping sweat from his face with a towel. He put the towel over his shoulders and looked at the cup with the cocoa stain in the bottom. "What about my cocoa?"

"It had turned too cool, sir. You wouldn't have liked it."

"That's good to know. . . . Solved the case for me yet?"

"I haven't actually had the chance to put my mind to it, but certain things seem obvious."

"Care to enlighten me? And maybe after that, you could fix a cup of cocoa."

"Oh, no, sir. One cup will hold me well enough. . . . As to the case at hand, it appears from your notes you believe there's a connection between the murders and the Manowack Indian Reservation near Cold Shepherd, and I think that makes sense. Sound reasoning, sir."

"Well, thank you, Alfred."

"Elementary."

"And what do you believe my next step will be, Mr. Holmes?"

"I presume you are planning to go to Cold Shepherd, sir. This . . . what is it . . . ?" Alfred looked at the printout. "Pale Boy. He might be quite an aid to you, having been born and raised on the reservation, and though that is an intelligent method of beginning your investigation, might I suggest you first go to the Gotham Boot and Leather Shop."

Bruce looked blank.

"Oh, the damage that could be fostered on your reputation if the public and the police department knew the assistance you required in solving your cases. . . . If you're having trouble following my line of reasoning, Master Bruce, please feel comfortable to ask questions at any time. I'm more than willing to accommodate you with my insights."

"Your suggestion has to do with the photo of the boot shop."

"Bravo. You deduced that because I'm now holding it in my heated little hand, I presume."

"You presume correct. . . . It's 'hot little hand,' Alfred. But I admit the exact connection between the photo and your excitement escapes me."

Alfred held up the photograph of the leather shop. He turned it toward Bruce. He positioned the magnifying glass over a portion of it. "If you examine the photo carefully, here in the shop, just visible with the magnifying glass—"

"Of course," Bruce said.

"You've slapped to it, sir?"

"Snapped, Alfred, not slapped. And yes, I know what you're driving at. . . . I *see* what you're driving at. Have I told you how smart you are lately?"

"Well, sir, I could quite do with more of it."

"You're smart, Alfred."

"Thank you, Master Bruce."

"I'll attend to your suggestion first thing."

"Very good, sir."

"Now, how about some breakfast, Alfred?"

Alfred rose and picked up the tray. "Oh, no, thank you, Master Bruce. I don't feel the least bit hungry. I ate early, and that cocoa seems to have topped me off nicely."

"Funny," Bruce said.

"Yes, sir. Laughter as the best medicine, and all that."

Alfred picked up the tray and empty cup and started for the steps that led to Wayne Manor.

"Just some oatmeal, Alfred?"

"Never bother the stuff, Master Bruce."

"Touch, Alfred. Never touch the stuff."

"Quite right, sir. Never do."

Alfred reached the top of the stairs, touched the spring lock with his foot, the wall slid back, and he stepped inside the clock. The wall closed behind him.

Clutch and Shift to—

[illegible]

[illegible]

[illegible]

[illegible]

[illegible]

[illegible]

[illegible]

[illegible]

[illegible]

[illegible]

[illegible]

—Fourth Gear

1

Cold Shepherd, Catherine Meadows's Hospital Office, Noon

Pale Boy leaned back in the leather office chair and looked slightly beyond Catherine Meadows, as if something profound lay to the side of and beyond her right ear. He said, "Doc, I feel funny about this."

"On the verge of laughter?"

"You know what I mean."

"That's why you won't look at me?"

"I feel like I'm at the principle's office or something."

"I'm worse than any principle. I'm a doctor. My closet is full of hacksaws and the shrunken heads of friends and clients."

Pale Boy tried to laugh, didn't make it entirely. He looked more like he'd prefer to chew glass.

"I want you to keep something in mind, Pale Boy."

"What's that?"

"You're not here in your underwear."

This time she got a real laugh from him, but a short one.

"All right, but I'm still nervous."

"Why?"

He examined a spider web in the upper corner of the room. "Mental problems, you know. I don't like to think about that. Talk about it. Get what I'm saying?"

"You're nuts, but would prefer people not know it?"

"Could be something like that. My grandfather may have been a lunatic. Misguided, anyway. I don't know. I just feel uncomfortable thinking I may have inherited it. Feel like I'm in a position of weakness. I'm more of a macho guy than I realized. Or I'm more involved with wanting to be thought that way than I realized. And coming here to talk about . . . these kind of things. I don't know, it makes me feel weak."

"Personally, Pale Boy, I've always seen you as a weenie. You coming here to talk to me about something that's bothering you, actually having a problem, well, that cinches it for me. I was right all along. You are a weenie. One of the biggest."

"Silly, huh?"

"*Stupid*'s more the word I had in mind. *Stupid* spelled with a big *S*. Listen here, Pale Boy. I'm not a practicing psychiatrist. I merely have the credentials. Besides, I don't fully trust psychiatry myself. Too many people think it's an exact science. Believe everything they're told. They use psychiatrists, analysts, therapists, to do coping they should do on their own. Love being told they're not at fault for anything. Personally, I believe in a little blame. We used to call it responsibility. Psychiatrists and therapists should be for major problems, not minor points of confusion. Those things are best discussed with a friend. Consider yourself talking to a friend. That shouldn't be difficult, should it? We're friends, aren't we?"

"I think so."

"Okay, the problems."

"I've had them before, but I thought I'd beaten them. I mean, they didn't seem like so much when I first had them, but they're coming back and I don't understand them exactly. They're stronger. I'm a little confused. It's not all mental. Some of it's physical."

"From the way you're rubbing your head, I assume the headaches haven't stopped?"

"They stop sometimes, for a little while. But lately they've become frequent. And very intense."

Catherine opened her desk drawer and took out a small bottle and opened it, poured out two pills. "Over-the-counter stuff, but pretty strong." She gave him the pills, walked over to the water cooler, plucked a paper cup from the rack, and filled it with water. She gave it to him. "Take those, then start at the top."

He took the pills, drank the water, wadded the cup, and tossed it in the trash can. "It goes back a ways."

"Then go back a ways. I get bored, I'll tell you."

"All right," he said, but didn't continue.

Catherine pulled the curtains, darkening the room. "Cozy, now, huh?" She sat behind her desk and opened the desk drawer again, put the headache tablets back and removed another bottle. Whiskey. "Hair of the dog?"

"No, thanks."

"I shouldn't, but what the hell?" She poured the cup full, sipped, shivered slightly. "That'll do it." She removed a cigarette wrapper and tobacco from her pocket, rapidly rolled a cigarette, stuck it in the corner of her mouth. She leaned back in the chair and put her feet on the desk. She had on socks with pink and gray clocks. Pale Boy found himself staring at them.

"Like 'em enough," she said, "I can show you where you can buy your own pair."

"Actually, I was wondering why you wear them. I had a pair like that, I'd keep them out of the public eye."

"You're trying to avoid what you came here for. You going to bore me or what?"

He nodded. "Okay, but I warn you, it's odd business."

"Odd business doesn't bother me. It's the waiting on the odd business bothers me. I could skip this, you know. Go on home. All I got there is a good dinner and a fine book to read, and heaven forbid I get a chance to do that, not when I can delight in sitting here waiting on you to talk to me."

"Anyone ever tell you that you were a bitch?"

"It comes up on a regular basis."

He smiled, then began to talk. "The hit-and-runs on Evan and Martha. I was going over my report this morning, and I might add, I've gotten the information back on the test results from Gotham."

"I've seen the autopsy reports on Martha. They were faxed to me. There are some inconsistencies there."

"The tire rubber taken from the street, the paint flecks on her body turning out to be blood and skin?"

"Yeah, but I'm not worked up about it. Mix-ups happen."

"Uh-huh, but I got one for you. I read in the newspaper about a similar hit-and-run in Gotham. I called the police department there, put a bug in their ear about our hit-and-run, pointed out similarities. They were ahead of me on it. They've even got that Batman guy involved."

"I know him. He's the best there is."

"What I'm getting at is the police over in Gotham sent me a report. The hit-and-run I read about, the test turned out the same. And when they told me the victim's name, I knew one of them . . . woman named Marilyn Cass. She was an anthropologist, worked in a museum there. Right before I went off to the army, she came to the reservation to do research on the Manowacks. The usual anthropological drivel. My brother Abner fell head over heels in love with her. Bad thing was he hated the whites, or was supposed to. That's what my grandfather taught us. Me, I just wanted to get away from that life, away from being an Indian."

"A little too much, you ask me."

"I don't think so. But she led him on, had a little fling with him, talked about love, whatever Abner wanted to hear, and when her job on the reservation was over, she went back to Gotham without so much as a go to hell. Used him. It made him even more bitter. Way he saw it, he'd fallen for a white trick, and he should have known better. Another treaty broken.

"Also, there was this salesman in Glendale. He was killed in his house—by a car. The evidence was, according to the police there, lost. I think it came up odd, like the Gotham hit-and-run, and they didn't know what to do with it. But this guy, Jerry Heilman, Abner knew him too. Like I knew him. I remember seeing his name on his shoe case. He was the man my mother ran off with. I've told you a little about that before."

Catherine nodded and Pale Boy continued.

"That was another white trick on Abner. Then there's me. We were close once, but he believes I gave in to the whites, and I'm worse than white to him. I'm an Uncle Tomahawk. I've betrayed everything he believes in, my grandfather believed in. I've gone the way of our father, and he hated him more than anyone."

"Abner knew Evan and Martha?"

"No, I believe that was a random attack, but it was a kind of revenge on me. I'm sheriff here, this is my town, and if there's one person he'd like to see suffer, slowly, it's me. I think there'll be other attacks, and eventually, I think it'll be me."

"Tell me more about your brother. About the two of you growing up on the reservation."

"Very well. And while I'm at it, I'll tell you about the cars and the shape-shifting."

"Shape-shifting?"

"I told you this was weird."

When Pale Boy finished an hour later, Catherine tossed her unlit cigarette in the trash can, smiled at him, and said, "You weren't just a woofin'. That story's strange, all right, but not to worry. I've heard nuttier in my time. Knew a guy once who was convinced he was a talking bisquit. You're only a little crazy, I think."

"That's reassuring," Pale Boy said. "Has a solid, professional ring to it. . . . What do you think? Really?"

"I think you may be on to something about your brother Abner being behind these murders. That he may have slipped a cog. But you really haven't any evidence, just circumstantial stuff, a feeling. You haven't even seen him lately. You don't even know he's up there. He may have left years ago."

"Not Abner. But you think it sounds likely, what I'm telling you?"

"That he may be behind the murders, yes. Connections are there. His knowing the woman murdered in Gotham, the shoe salesman being the man your mother ran off with. . . . I'm sorry, I put that bluntly."

"It's all right."

"Maybe too all right, Pale Boy. You seem to contain your anger a little too well."

"Who says I'm angry? What is, is."

"It's not that easy. But, to continue the line of thought, those murders, the attacks here in the town to have revenge on you. It makes a kind of sense. Too many coincidences for there not to be something to it . . . but you haven't actually had contact with Abner since you were a young man, and to think that he's . . . Well, the method sounds, shall we say, a little too much."

"What about the lab tests coming up blood and skin?"

"But shape-shifting?"

"An old Manowack tradition, actually."

"Into cars? I doubt it."

"Shape-shifting is shape-shifting. I think I've come to the conclusions Abner did. Cars are what he loved, that's where he saw the true source of power, and that's what shape-shifting Manowack style is about. Recognizing the sources of power and flowing into them. My grandfather, for all his strength, may have finally weakened. He may have seen the handwriting on the wall, or perhaps I should say skywriting. He didn't really feel powerful anymore.

What's a wolf compared to a car when it comes to pure, raw power? So, at the core, he lost his belief, and now my brother has gained a new belief. . . . Man, listen to me."

"You should hear it from this end."

"Catherine, what I'm telling you, I don't believe it either. The rational part of me doesn't, anyway. The part that's grown up on white man's logic. But the Indian part of me does. A saying among the Manowack is that no Indian will say he believes in the supernatural these days, but he won't say he doesn't either. I'm an exception. I said I didn't, and maybe I was wrong. Maybe I lied to myself . . . I don't know. I'm not wanting you to say, 'Yeah, you're right, Pale Boy, your brother is shape-shifting into a Ford Thunderbird.' I don't want that at all."

"You won't get it either. Spread your ears and take this in: I don't think people change into cars, animals, birds, trees, or rocks. They change their clothes and their ways, not into critters or automobiles. Read my lips: Your brother may be behind this, but if he is, he's doing it with a car, he is not a car."

"And my dreams about the hanging boy?"

"Haven't got a clue on that one. Tell you what, let me think about it, not as a friend, but as a psychiatrist."

"I leave out of here, you're going to call the men in the little white coats, right?"

"Immediately. . . . Hell, no! This is confidential between us. You leave, I'll give this stupid story some serious thought—"

"Don't try so hard to build my confidence."

"—and I'll call you."

Pale Boy stood up. "Thanks. I think."

Catherine opened her desk drawer and took the bottle of tablets out of it and handed it to him. "Take 'em. Instructions are on the bottle. Follow them. I'm going to call downstairs, arrange for an X ray of your skull. Go down there and get it done."

"Whatever you say, Mom." He put the pills in his pocket and they shook hands. He went out and closed the door.

Catherine picked up the phone, arranged for the X ray, made some more calls.

An hour later she went downstairs to the fax machine and received the information she had asked for: Pale Boy's educational, military, and medical records. She went by and picked up the X rays.

She packed them in a folder with the other records, made some room visits, thumped some chests, and checked some charts; then she took the file, checked out for the day, and drove home.

She ate cold pizza, retired to her study, and cracked the folder on Pale Boy and yawned. The hours were getting to her. She thought about the story Pale Boy had told her and shook her head. It wasn't a professional thing to consider, and she liked Pale Boy so much, but maybe, just maybe, he was nuts.

The records she had requested were more extensive than the ones she had seen before, back when she gave Pale Boy his city employee examination.

Leaning back in her chair, she put on her glasses and began to read. One item in the army report struck her like a missile. She read it again. She hastily made notes.

When she finished, she reached in her desk drawer with a shaky hand and got out her home bottle of whiskey and poured a fresh drink and rolled a cigarette. She put the cigarette in her mouth, twisted it from one side of her lips to the other, and this time, for the first time in ages, and without thinking, she found her lighter and lit it. She read the report through again.

"Ho boy," she said. She checked her watch and made a phone call, crushed out the last of her cigarette and lit another.

2

The Cave Beneath Wayne Manor, 4:00 P.M.

He hated going out in the daylight and usually avoided it at all cost. In the daytime the uniform didn't work as effectively. His power lay in the night and the mystery of the night; there, shrouded in darkness, he was Batman.

But Alfred was right about the photograph. You looked at it closely, through the picture window across the way, you could see the glint of a little silver object hanging from the ceiling of the shop, an object that under a magnifying glass was the lens of an in-store surveillance camera. It would be the type of camera that rotated and at times pointed to the front glass of the store, and that meant it pointed into the street. Perhaps—just perhaps—the assault in the alley had been recorded on it.

So after breakfast—Alfred had prepared one for him after all, but not without grumbling—he surveyed his notes, analyzed his dream, and kicked it all around again and again. He didn't like what it was pointing to.

He burned off some tension on the parallel bars and the punching bag, then decided, day or no day, he had to pursue what the evidence suggested he pursue.

Slipping on his uniform, he got in the Batmobile and checked the dash monitors, saw there was no one on the road outside of the cave's secret exit. He activated the facade of brush and rocks with a switch beneath the dash, gunned the motor and went out of the cave and into the daylight, turned onto the main road. He drove midtown to the station, went up and talked to Gordon, got him to request that the Boot and Leather Shop turn over to him its surveillance video recorded on the date of the hit-and-run.

Gordon called the shop and Batman drove over there.

"Nothing in it will help," said the proprietor of Boot and Leather, a little guy who looked as if he had been soaked in grease and hung out to dry. "I seen it already. I look at 'em now and then, and there was a murder on it, I'd have called in and said so. Know what I'm saying?"

"I'd care to look at it just the same," Batman said.

"Yeah, sure. Watch it in health. Come on back."

Batman followed to the desk in the rear and the little man removed a videocassette from a drawer and put it on the desk. Batman reached for it.

"Wait a minute," he said. "That ain't the one. That's a tape of me and the ol' lady, know what I'm saying? Things get dull, no customers in the store, I pop it in the VCR in the back there, watch a little personal action. Beats another Rambo movie. I can make you a dub if you want."

"No, thanks."

"Better than you'd think. I'm not so bad setting up a camera. Not too sloppy at the rest of it, either—neither's the ol' lady, know what I mean?"

"I know what you mean. But no, thanks."

"Hey, you had the opportunity, right?"

"Regret sets in, I know who to call."

"There you are."

The little man removed the cassette, pulled out a stack of them, and put them on the desk. "Let me see here. I don't think I taped over that one. Thing too is I keep the movies I watch up here with 'em, you know. Usually tape over the store videotapes after I take a look at 'em. Like to see who's walking by here at night. Get a good view of the front window with the camera, you know. Someone comes by regular, looks like they're casing the joint, I can sort of watch for 'em they come in, know what I'm saying?"

The little man sorted through the tapes. Some of them had titles stickered to their sides: *Bambi*; *Evil Dead*; *Gandhi*; *Our Christmas Vacation in Mexico City*; *Fifth Wedding Anniversary*.

"Yeah, here it is. I got to have the tape back or some money for it, though. They ain't giving these things away, you know."

Batman removed a bill from one of his belt pouches and put it on the desk.

"That gets it," said the little man. He palmed the bill, popped it between his hands, squinted his eyes, and held it to the light. "Counterfeit bucks comes in now and then. Can't be too sure. Not saying you'd pass one, you know, but you could get one passed to you."

"That a fact?"

"Hey, happens to the best of us."

Satisfied, the little man shoved the bill into his pants pocket. "Hey, let me ask you a personal question, all right?"

"Ask."

"That bat suit? It hot, or what?"

"Sometimes," Batman said, and he picked up the cassette and left the store.

Back in the cave, he removed the Batman uniform and pulled on his workout pants; then he slipped the cassette into the voice-activated video computer, sat before the motion picture–sized screen, and watched. It was pretty dull stuff. Various views of the store. None of the boots walked and none of the leather formed itself into a cow. Few people strolled by the picture window.

Then he saw shadowy movement beyond the window. Shapes were moving into frame on the sidewalk across the street, moving swiftly. That far away, the camera's focus was weak. Bruce spoke to the computer.

"Freeze frame."

The computer froze the cassette's position.

"Lighten and enlarge."

The screen lightened and became full of something too close to identify.

"Left-center image to the center of the screen. Half power."

What he saw now were a man and a woman, and he recognized them from their "before" photos—Harders McCammon and Marilyn Cass.

"Continue."

The camera swung slowly to the right, leaving the couple. The camera filled with the contents of the store, swung to the rear of it, and after what seemed a millennium, rotated forward. The couple hadn't moved, but now only the tops of their heads were visible over the roof of a car, a black Thunderbird.

They were staring at the car. Gradually they began to move; then the car moved, whipped to the left, and the couple broke and ran into the mouth of the alley. The Thunderbird followed. Only its taillights were visible after that.

"Magnify central image. Slow mo and advance."

What Batman saw sickened him. He only thought he had seen everything. The car worked the couple like a cat playing with mice. It made impossible turns. Sometimes, to make a turn in the tight alleyway, it looked like a dog turning to bite its tail. Cars couldn't do that. Metal didn't do that. Nothing Bruce knew in this universe could do that.

By the time the thief came into the alley and found Harders McCammon's leg and hit him with it, his actions seemed almost normal.

Bruce ran the tape back, saw the same thing, turned it off.

He found a map of Cold Shepherd, turned his remarkable concentration up to high, memorized the streets and the location of major buildings as fast as he could read them. He put his uniform on again, started up the Batmobile, left the cave, set the car's nose in the direction of Cold Shepherd.

to the rear of [illegible], with [illegible]
moved forward. The people [illegible]
in [illegible]
[illegible]

They [illegible]. Gradually [illegible]
[illegible]

[illegible]

[illegible]

He found a map of [illegible]
concentrating [illegible] up to [illegible] memorized the streets and the
locations of major buildings [illegible].
He put [illegible] uniform [illegible] started up the [illegible]
left the car [illegible] the direction of [illegible]
[illegible]

3

From *The Book of the Thunderbird*, Date Recorded, Unknown

Dead so far, five little white folks.

And soon to come: ONE LITTLE INDIAN BOY.

Watch out, bubba, 'cause here I come, my pressure plate's burning and I'm riding the clutch.

Udden, udden.

4

6:00 P.M.

After leaving Catherine, Pale Boy drove around town, making his rounds but not really seeing much. His thoughts were turned inward. His head hurt something awful. He was tempted to drive out to the Pyramid of Cars and see if Abner was there, confront him. But he hesitated. The time was not right for that. What could he say to him after all these years? *Howdy. Been a while. By the way, are you turning into a Thunderbird to get even with me?* And if he was, what could Pale Boy do about it?

His memory of shape-shifting told him that a shape-shifter could be hurt, but not easily. Inconsequential wounds would heal quickly. For that matter, unless the shape-shifter was completely destroyed and his soul was given up to the Owl God, he could repair most any damage done to him while in the shape-shifter state. Previous wounds were a weakness—a bum knee, for instance. That would be the shape-shifter's weak point even in his transformed state.

Pale Boy tried to remember if Abner had any physical weak points, but couldn't remember one. He found that he could hardly remember Abner at all.

As night neared, the idea of shape-shifting became more real to him. And his head hurt something ferocious. He began to think of Angie and how she could be in the middle of all this. He was supposed to relieve Herkemer shortly, but the more he thought of Angie, the more he felt it necessary to talk to her, to warn her, even if she thought he was loony as a cartoon. He could apologize and explain to Herkemer a little later, make up the time he stole from him.

He drove home.

When he came in and closed the door, Angie appeared from her studio holding a paintbrush. She was covered in paint. "I wasn't expecting you this early," she said.

"I know. I'm not feeling well." He tossed his hat on the couch.

"Cold?"

"Headaches."

"Still? Honey, you should see a doctor about that."

"Just did. Catherine gave me some pills."

"Good. Anything I can do for you?"

"Talk."

"Sure, let me clean up."

"No. We can go in your studio. You want, you can paint while I talk."

They went into the studio. Darkness was beginning to fill the room. Angie reached for the light string and tugged the light on. She sat down on her stool in front of the canvas containing the Pyramid of Cars. She was still working on it. Pale Boy stared at it. It seemed even more foreboding than before. A bead of sweat broke over an eyebrow and coasted over his eyelid and fell, splashed onto his cheek. He felt as if his insides were spinning. The danging light bulk struck him as exceptionally bright, and the moonlight in the painting pulsed, made his eyes hot and feverish.

"You look serious," Angie said. "You're scaring me a little."

He smiled, feeling as if his face might crack with the effort. "I don't mean to scare you. You've got nothing to be scared of. Well, yes, you do. Not from me, of course—"

"I never thought to be scared of you."

"—but Abner, maybe."

"Abner?"

"My brother."

"Brother? You never told me you had a brother. Long as we've been together, you never said anything about a brother."

"Not only do I have one, I think he's a brick shy a load. I think he could be dangerous, and I fear because of me, you're in danger. And something else: I never told you about my father either." He nodded at her painting. "The Pyramid of Cars. My family owned it."

"What?"

"Still owns it. Abner does, anyway. My father ran it when I was growing up."

"You should have told me, baby. Does my painting it somehow distress you?"

Pale Boy rubbed his head, found a stool and sat.

"Maybe. I don't know, really. I feel kind of detached from my whole past. Like I didn't really live it. Like I read about it. Know what I'm saying?"

"I think so."

"No. No, you don't. You couldn't. I don't mean that like it sounds, Angie. It's just that I'm . . . well, I'm confused. I've been having bad dreams. This hit-and-run business seems to be part of it, but the headaches . . . I haven't had them like this in a long time. Not since I got my head busted. I told you about that. And this dream I'm having, it makes no sense to me. Yet somehow I feel it should. Hell, I'm not sure I know what I'm saying."

"It's okay, baby. Just take it slow and explain. Start at the beginning."

5

Events Beginning 6:58 P.M.

Batman passed the Pyramid of Cars.

As he passed, he turned his head to see the sun, a rotting plum going soft at the bottom, dripping into the mountains, leaking juice onto the pile of rust, making it appear blood red. Night's first shadows began to creep down from the mountain range like grim reapers.

As he drove, Batman considered his dream, its car motif. He mentally reviewed the video from Gotham Boot and Leather. Linking the video with his dream, he was certain now he knew what was going on. His dream and his subconscious were ahead of his rationale. They were telling him what his logic wanted to deny.

He put his foot to the floorboard. The black dart of a car leapt forward.

With the last rot of the plum-sun soaking into the mountains, the shadows crawling out of their day graves, he raced the Batmobile into Cold Shepherd, and on over to the Sheriff's office.

When Batman entered, Herkemer, who was sitting behind his desk with a magazine turned sideways and a foldout dangling from it, stopped checking Miss August's anatomy and put the magazine on the desk. He cranked his bottom jaw up and swallowed.

"My God . . . you're the real one? Batman?"

"One of one," Batman said. "Is Sheriff Pale Boy in?"

"No, he said he was going to go over to see Dr. Meadows . . . over at the hospital . . . Cupp Street, you can't miss it—"

"I know where it is. I memorized a map before I came."

"Oh, well, yeah, okay . . . I can't believe it. Batman."

"I'll go over there, then. I miss him, tell him I'll catch up with him later."

"Yeah, sure—I mean, whatever. There's just the one of you, right? Not a bunch of guys who do the stuff they say you do?"

"No one does all the stuff they say I do. But yes, like I said, I'm one of one."

"That thing with the guy called himself Two Face. That story in the *Gotham Times*—"

"You mean Harvey Dent. It was exaggerated. Goodbye for now, Deputy."

"Yeah, okay . . . sure. Bye . . . for now. Hey, hey, wait a minute!" Herkemer looked at his watch. "Time it is, Meadows would have gone on home. Fact is, Pale Boy's supposed to have relieved me by now so I can eat some dinner. No telling where he is."

"Doctor Meadows's address?"

"Raisor Street. Biggest house there, got a lot of oaks

around. I guess Raisor Street's on the map you memorized?"

"It is."

Batman turned to leave.

"Hey, you see Pale Boy, tell him I need to eat something. I'm so hungry I'm starting to see hamburgers walking on the ground."

"I will," Batman said, and he went out and closed the door.

Herkemer went to the window, watched the big man get in a dark-looking car at the curb. He thought, *The Batmobile. It really is him. Man, wait till Karen hears about this. But one guy, I don't know. One guy would be awful busy to do all he does. Got to be a bunch of them with matching suits.*

The door to the Batmobile closed. Batman was no longer visible. The tinted glass and the dripping night took care of that.

The car edged away from the curb into the thickening dusk.

Herkemer ran to the phone, dialed hastily, vibrated on the balls of his feet while he waited for it to ring.

When the phone was picked up on the other end he spoke immediately. "Hey, you won't guess who just came in here. Go ahead, give it a guess."

"Jack the goddamn Ripper. Who is this?"

"Oh, I'm sorry, sir. Wrong number."

He hung up and dialed more carefully.

The phone rang.

And rang.

No one was home.

Herkemer hung up. "Typical."

6

Fully night now.

The house on Raisor Street looked Gothic, lights like yellow cat eyes behind two windows. A great oak in the front yard nodded its limbs in the wind.

Batman parked at the curb.

Catherine made some hasty notes on her notepad. She turned on her desk lamp. And there across from her was a shape. She let out a yell and snatched up the whiskey bottle on her desk: whiskey gurgled onto the floor and into her lap as she cocked it over her shoulder.

"Catherine. Good to see you."

"Damn you, Batman."

"Sorry. I couldn't resist."

"What you think I got a lock on my door for?"

"It wasn't locked."

Catherine put the whiskey bottle on the desk. "What do you think it's closed for?"

"Habits die hard."

"Yeah, well, go on and kill them. Don't come sneaking around in my house. You knock on the door, phone, or something. How long you been standing there?"

"Long enough to know you still drink too much and to see you have medical records of Cold Shepherd's sheriff on your desk."

"Not just medical. Pull up a chair and sit down. You could have said something, you know, not just stand there. I might have been picking my nose or something. Drink?"

He pulled up a chair and sat down. "No, thanks. And you shouldn't either."

"I keep it under control."

"I've heard that before. From you, in Gotham."

"I left Gotham because I wanted to leave. Not because of the whiskey. The pressure got to me."

"Whatever you say."

"I wasn't drinking that much. I'm not an alcoholic or anything."

"You're functional, but you're an alcoholic. . . . I didn't come here to argue your private life with you, though. I'm here about the hit-and-run murders."

Catherine screwed the cap on the whiskey bottle. "I've kind of been expecting you. Called Gordon the other day about the autopsy, and about transferring Evan to Gotham. He said he was going to pull you in on this business. I assumed it had to be something special."

"I presume you don't know about Evan?"

"What?"

"He was murdered in the hospital."

Catherine sat stunned. She looked at the materials on her desk. "I don't like the way all this is coming together.

In spite of what I know, I don't like what the evidence is pointing to."

"What do you know?"

She broke out her cigarette papers and tobacco. "You can quit looking at me like I'm biting heads off puppies. I'm not going to smoke it. First two I've had in a while were today, after reading this. Smoked them before I knew it. Normally I hold them in my mouth. Gives me courage."

She finished rolling the smoke and put it in the corner of her mouth. The cigarette made a couple of trips from one side of her mouth to the other. She talked around it. "Figure since it wasn't a professional visit I can talk about it. . . . Well, I got to talk about it. Friendly, professional, or what. Sheriff here, Pale Boy—"

"I know of him."

"He's been having some problems. Came in today to talk. Told me about some headaches he's been having. Got banged when he was an M.P., breaking up a bar fight. Been having visions of someone hanging, some kid he felt he should know but couldn't recognize. X rays I had him take today, they look bad. The place in his head, the skull's separated."

"That's affecting him?"

"Damn sure isn't helping him. He thinks his brother, Abner, is behind the killings, and he had some good reasons for thinking it, though nothing concrete. Circumstantial stuff. But he started talking about shape-shifting, and that isn't the whole of it. Not turning into wolves, stuff like that, but turning into—"

"Cars. A Thunderbird, perhaps?"

Catherine's cigarette fled from one corner of her mouth to the other. "How'd you figure that?"

"I'm a trained detective."

"But you're not a humorist."

"I saw where Evan died. I said that he was murdered, but I didn't say how. He was on the fourth floor of the hospital. His room looked like a car had been there. That made no sense, but the evidence was contrary to that. Then there's the blood samples. You know about that. And there's a videotape." He told her about the videotape.

Catherine nodded. "I don't know I can believe this."

"It makes no difference what you believe; it's happening, Catherine. Indian magic tied in with technology goes along with what you were telling me about Pale Boy, what he was saying about Abner."

"Uh-huh. Only there's a catch. Those records I got today. One of them was from the Manowack Reservation office. It's more detailed about Pale Boy's past than the army records. There isn't any Abner. There was, but he died when Pale Boy was eleven. Right after their grandfather died."

"Pale Boy had to know."

"He knew, all right. He found him. Way I read it, Abner couldn't take the duality of worlds—Indian and white. Took some battery cables and automotive wiring, made a noose, and hung himself inside the Pyramid of Cars. That's a place—"

"I know what it is."

"Pale Boy struck me as talking a little too removed about his father, brother, and grandfather. According to these records, he'd been seeing a shrink in the army. Guy helping him cope with this white–Indian thing. Then, as an M.P., he got his head knocked, but good. That put him out of the army, and I think that old wound, combined with the guilt he feels about Abner has brought back some repressed memories, like the ability to shape-change. The belief that he once knew how to do it.''

''Someone knows how.''

''But to make those memories palatable to the progressive Pale Boy, his mind has to have Abner alive, an adult, living on the reservation, on the car lot with the Pyramid of Cars. Abner takes care of all of Pale Boy's repressed hostility, his confusion.

''Add that to the guilt he feels about his father, wanting to love him, wanting to please him and be white, and then his mother running off with a white man, dying away from home, and him never really seeing her dead, allowing himself to feel her loss . . . well, we've got a guy that's pretty confused.''

''And the blow to the head may have confused him even more?''

''That's how I figure. This woman he told me Abner had an affair with, the lady who was killed—''

''It wasn't Abner who had the affair, it was Pale Boy.''

''Looks likely. Guy with her was just in the wrong place at the wrong time. And the shoe salesman who was killed was the man that ran off with Pale Boy's mother, and as sheriff, him having access to so many records and files, it wouldn't have been difficult for him to look Heilman up and hunt him down. Kill him however he killed him. Victims here in Cold Shepherd were just victims. It was the Abner side of Pale Boy trying to get even with his brother. Only they're both the same man. Sounds wild, dual personality and all, but it makes sense. . . . 'Course, you know a little about dual personalities yourself, don't you?''

"I believe I do."

"I made a call to the reservation office on an off chance of catching someone after hours, and did. Pale Boy still owns that lot. Man I talked to, tribal representative, he said Pale Boy still owns it, but no one runs it anymore. Said many Manowacks think it's haunted. I asked him if he did, and he said no, but he also said he didn't go up there either. Kids don't even go there to play. But I think when Pale Boy becomes Abner he goes there, then when he's Pale Boy he has no memory of it. As for him shape-shifting into an automobile, I don't care if you think that's happening and he thinks it, I don't buy it. Not even if the two of you told me he was turning into something as benign as a hamster."

"I'm not trying to sell it to you, Catherine. But if everything is made of molecules—human flesh, cars—if shape-shifting is possible at all, there's no reason it can't apply to inanimate objects. I've seen some unusual things in my career, enough so I can believe most anything if the evidence is there, and I think it's there. You see the video I saw, and it'll change your mind."

"Perhaps."

"It's a moot point at the moment. But you will agree Pale Boy's dangerous? He's not in control?"

"That I agree with."

"According to his deputy, he didn't return to his office after seeing you. Give Herkemer a call. See if he's there."

"Very well." Catherine called, got Herkemer, spoke to him briefly, hung up.

"Still hasn't seen him. And he's supposed to have been in long ago. He said if we see Pale Boy, tell him he's hungry."

"I believe the best idea is for me to pay Pale Boy a visit."

Catherine's face suddenly changed. "Angie . . . his girlfriend. They live together. Way he's acting, getting more and more erratic . . . If he's gone home and Abner makes an appearance . . . We've got to get over there."

"We?"

"You could use someone with you who knows him and knows something about psychology. Besides, I stay here, I'll just drink. And you don't take me, you'll have to get the address somewhere else."

"Do you ever tire of playing the 'tough ol' broad' role?"

"Never."

Push On into—

—Overdrive

1

"So you see, Angie, I'm confused. All this stuff with my past, jumbling up . . . my headaches." Pale Boy rose from the stool and began to pace, trying to find more words, trying to get out what was inside him, but feeling as if he were fishing for it without bait. As he paced, he turned and saw the mirror across the way, the painting in its reflection, Angie, his white woman, turning on her stool to follow his movement. He could see himself too. Or what should be himself. But wasn't. Abner was standing there instead, standing in front of the mirror in the exact same pose as he was, only with a braid of automotive wires and battery cables noosed around his neck. He hadn't seen Abner in years, but that's who it was. He knew immediately. Why was he wearing that noose? He wanted desperately for Abner to move so he could see his own face in the mirror. He wanted that and didn't know why.

But Abner wouldn't move. Couldn't move. He wasn't standing in front of the mirror, after all. He was *in* the mirror, filling the space where Pale Boy knew his reflection should be.

He turned to Angie and pointed a finger. "See! See!"

Angie looked in the mirror. She saw herself, the painting, the room, and Pale Boy pointing his finger at his image in the mirror.

"Abner, you bastard!" Pale Boy wheeled back to face the mirror, jumped forward and kicked the man in the glass. Cracks, like a road map of highways, filled the mirror and pieces burst from it and clattered to the floor.

Angie leapt from her stool and screamed, "Pale Boy! What are you doing?"

Pale Boy turned and glared at her. His face looked . . . wrong. Darker.

"White tramp!" he said.

"Baby . . ."

"Don't baby me. That's what she did. Marilyn. She called me baby. But she didn't mean it any more than you."

"What are you talking about? Pale Boy, please don't play like this. It isn't funny."

"She just wanted to have fun with the Indian. Mock me. Like you mock that idiot Pale Boy, calling him Tonto."

"You're scaring me. Please stop."

"Pale Boy, he can stand that kind of thing, likes it."

"Honey . . . what's wrong?"

"But me, once burned, I don't get burned again."

"Easy, baby. We can talk about it." But even as Angie tried to reason, she knew he was beyond it. Something alien had descended on him, as though seeping in through the ache in his head, and though she had never thought to be scared of him, she was scared now. She eyed the door to the left of Pale Boy, wondered if she could scoot past him and make it.

"I know what you're thinking," he said. "I can see it in your white woman eyes. . . . You can't get past me, tramp."

Pale Boy stretched on his toes and reached to the ceiling. When he lowered his arms his face wobbled and jerked violently. And then it broadened, the bones growing beneath his skin, the skin stretching to accommodate it, turning darker, darker. His gums and teeth, as if on extensions, shoved his lips apart and protruded a full foot from Pale Boy's mouth. The teeth gleamed silver and were suddenly metallic, like automotive grillwork—grillwork expanding on both sides of Pale Boy's mouth, growing so wide and large and heavy, he was forced to bend double. His head dove forward and the grillwork clanked on the concrete floor with a flurry of sparks. He shot out his clenched fist and slammed his knuckles on the floor before him, as if preparing to do pushups on them. His fists ballooned dramatically, turned the color of ripe eggplants.

Angie stumbled backwards, knocking over the painting of the Pyramid of Cars. What she saw she couldn't be seeing. It wasn't possible. She snatched up the stool to defend herself, because there was nowhere to run.

The impossible continued.

The street where Pale Boy and Angie lived was not far from Catherine Meadows's residence. Batman and Catherine drove over in five minutes. It was a nice neighborhood, houses well spaced from one another on huge well-mowed lawns spotted with oaks.

The house they wanted was a simple affair. White and blue, mostly dark. One spot of light was visible through a crack in a front window curtain, glowing from somewhere in the back of the house, like a single coal in a furnace.

Pale Boy's fists were now large as tires. In fact, they *were* tires. The cracks between his clenched fingers had become wide treads. His boots split and his feet curled, toes to heels, knotting, darkening, swelling swiftly into tires, ankle bones turning into shiny hubs. His clothes, shirt, pants, and underwear popped away from him and fluttered in all directions, as if vomited from an abusive dryer.

His grillwork teeth pounded on the floor as Pale Boy's broadening neck tried to lift his head, but couldn't manage. Spittle flew from between the bars of the grillwork and struck the ground and turned the cherry-black color of transmission fluid. A groan rose out of him, mutated into the rumble of a powerful V-8. Ribs fanned and buttocks spread. His dark hair expanded like stain across his head, covered his body, and went lacquer-hard. His eyes punched from their sockets as if being poked from behind by fingers. They jelly-wobbled, dilated. The pupils exploded into five pieces and swirled around the edges of the whites. The fragments resembled faceless human shapes flailing against the inside of the eyeballs; a faint squeaking came from them, like mice trapped behind glass. The eyes widened and hardened and turned bright—headlights.

His neck was wide, and now the bones above his headlights popped and rocked and stretched and became a hood, his forehead a windshield. His shoulders dipped and broadened, and the hump of his back went up and met the swell of the neck and kept rising, became the roof, dipped off toward the buttocks, which had lengthened and spread, and streamlined into the rear of a Thunderbird.

Finished now, the flesh engine purred and rumbled and stood on its hind tires and waved its front tires in the air like a performing horse.

And the Thunderbird leapt forward and came down on top of Angie and her pathetic stool with a crunch. Blood spewed, rode up the treads of the tires, then flew away from them, freckled the walls. A wisp of blackness swirled out of Angie and ducked into the bright headlights of the Thunderbird, swirled temporarily, formed a little human silhouette inside each lamp, raced around their circumference before crumbling apart like burnt gingerbread. There was a flicker behind the Thunderbird's dark windshield. It let out a sigh.

Batman closed the door to the Batmobile just as Catherine was climbing out on her side, and at the same moment they heard the roar of an engine. The front door of the house bulged and popped into the yard like a wine cork. It was followed by the wall and a sleek black Thunderbird, its horn honking, its radio wailing "Hot Rod Lincoln."

It raced by them, wearing wallpaper and plaster like mink and accessories, hit the street, made an impossible left with such violence the wallpaper and the plaster lost their positions and took to the sky. The Thunderbird roared away, leaving them with its red taillights to stare at until they too receded into the night. Plaster sprinkled Batman and Catherine like snow and wallpaper coasted left, right, left, right, and crumpled into the yard.

The front of the house groaned, lumber sighed, and the roof leaned forward as if it were a peaked hat sliding off a drunk witch's head. But it didn't give all the way. From the interior came threatening squeaks.

Batman raced through the gap where the doorway had been. A board swung out as he passed, clattered to the ground. The living room was a mess, television, VCR, end table smashed flat. The car had shoved the couch out of its path and hard against the wall, bringing a knick-knack shelf down onto its cushions. The floor was littered with glass and wood and plaster.

Through a doorway, in a room beyond, a naked bulb swung back and forth on a cord. Shadows danced.

Batman moved into the room and took a look. Paint was splattered everywhere and so was blood. On the floor was a vaguely human shape, only made out of mashed silly putty and splattered with tomatoes.

Behind him came a snapping of wood, a crunching of glass.

Without looking at her, Batman said, "You might prefer not to look, Catherine. Even a doctor can't help here."

"Too late," she said at his shoulder. "And I'm not about to become a shrinking violet now."

2

Catherine bent over what had been Angie. "He loved her," she said. "I really believe that."

"But Abner didn't," Batman said.

"He was jealous and Pale Boy is jealous of him for his loyalty to the Manowack. Culture collision. Pale Boy thinks he wants out of being an Indian, but he really wants in. And when he's Abner, he thinks he wants in, but he really wants out."

"You said his father owned the Pyramid of Cars?"

"Yes." She laughed in a way that didn't sound at all amused. "He really is turning into a car, isn't he? It was me, I'd want to be a refrigerator. I like to eat. . . . Jesus, what am I saying?"

Catherine turned her head from Angie's remains. The room was filled with the stench of death, burned rubber and wisps of exhaust. She pulled the stink in and blew it out her nostrils, hard, as if the action could clear the odors from the room. She saw something, reached out and touched it. She shoved the fragments of a stool aside and brushed off some wall plaster. She pulled the bent and tire-burned painting Angie had been working on out of the debris and looked at it. "The Pyramid of Cars," she said.

But when she turned the painting toward Batman, he was gone.

"Dark ghost, try not to hurt him," she said.

3

The Batmobile hummed through the darkness toward the Pyramid of Cars. After all that Catherine had told him, it seemed logical to Batman that the pyramid was where Pale Boy would go. It contained all his connections, white and Indian, automotive and supernatural.

When the car jetted over a hill and the pyramid came into sight, it looked different. The moonlight was diluted and tarnished by a roll of thin but dark clouds. The lunar rays slipped through the clouds and bathed the structure and made it look like an enormous heap of copper-colored corpses, and something moved atop the mound like a squirming maggot.

Pale Boy.

As he pulled off the highway and onto the road that led to the lot, there was a sound like thunder, combined with a lightning strike.

* * *

Pale Boy stopped crushing cars. He put the remote on his knee, swiveled the chair, and watched the strange dark car ride the red clay ribbon that wound up to the lot. He was amazed he couldn't identify its type. Looked a little like a Chevy Camaro, but not exactly. A customized job. Sounded good. Special engine. It was the dark car he had seen outside of Pale Boy's house. Seemed too that he had seen a woman there, and a man/bird. The Owl God, perhaps. The one in whose shadow you dare not walk.

Or perhaps he had imagined that. Things were sort of confused. He couldn't lock onto his thoughts. They seemed to have wandered off, gone on vacation. He remembered seeing his brother at the house, of that he was certain, and the blond girl, and he remembered killing them, smashing them with his fists . . . his tires.

He swiveled completely around as the dark car finished off the road and wound around and among the rusting car bodies and halted below the pyramid. The lights went dead. The motor stopped. The door opened. A man got out—no, not a man. A thing both man and bird. It was the Owl God, come by automobile. Well, that made sense.

He picked up the remote and punched it. One of half a dozen cars lined up on the track slid forward into the saddle and was crunched and smashed and spat out at the other end, a block of metal. He punched off the crusher, looked down. The Owl God was leaning on the door of his car, looking up. He yelled, "Pale Boy!"

Nice, he thought. The thing he hated the most, his brother, and he had been mistaken for him. By the Owl God, no less. Once the white man set things on a bad course, those things really went downhill at an accelerated rate.

He sat silent for a moment, then moved the chair slightly with his foot, pushed again, creaked it back to its former position. He looked up and through the black, gossamer veil of clouds at the slash of moon. He tried to will its light into his head. It seemed to him that if he could fill the crack in his head with moonlight, it would glue him together and the agony would cease. But it wasn't working. The moonlight paid absolutely no attention. It wouldn't flow into him. He lowered his head and looked at the Owl God, said, "My brother, the Uncle Tomahawk, he was Pale Boy. He's dead. Why do you call me that?"

"You are Pale Boy."

"We didn't look that much alike. Don't call me his name. Call me Abner."

"Abner's dead. Been dead these long years. You're not Abner."

"Oh, I'm Abner, all right."

"Catherine Meadows, you remember her, don't you?"

A pause. "No."

"You spoke to her today about your problems."

"No. Leave me alone. My head hurts. I don't believe you're the Owl God. I believe you're the trickster."

"I'm neither. I'm a man. A dual man, like you. You're not in control. I can get you help. Make you better."

"Help? You can bring back the old ways? You can take the car out of my heart and give me back the wolf and the hawk?"

"No. But I know people that can help you adjust to change."

"Adjust to it! You want me to adjust to it? That's the white answer to everything. Adjust. No more animals. The wolf and the coyote smashed beneath the wheels of a truck. The hawk, dead from eating poisoned mice, diseased rabbits. Sorry, have to adjust. Progress, you know. Rivers and creeks are full of garbage and sewage. Damn, what a shame. Adjust. Air's polluted with car exhausts and crap from smokestacks. It stinks and tastes funny, and you can't see the stars some nights, hardly see the moon. Adjust. The cities, there's an example of progress. Crime. Hunger. Hate. . . ."

"You're full of hate. You don't have to—"

"Yes. I'm full of hate. Bitterness. This was ours. The Manowacks'. The ignorant savages who had their own language and government, lived in harmony with nature, and then along came white people. They not only polluted the earth, they polluted the minds of the Manowacks. The Manowacks want to be like white people now. TVs humming. Video games hopping. Big Cadillacs rolling. Soda pop and cupcakes for breakfast. I know, I'm that way. I hate it! I hate me! I hate them! I hate us! Technology wins all. Technology owns all. The wolf, the hawk, the owl, they have no power in this world. Money. Technology. The smokestack. The fast, sleek car, a quick burger and fries pushed out of a window at you, the sound of rock 'n' roll. That's where the power is."

"Come down."

"Oh, I'll come down, all right." Pale Boy/Abner grabbed the remote from his knee and tossed it at Batman. It missed, hit the ground, and skidded. Pale Boy/Abner stood. "I'll come down on your head!"

* * *

Batman thought, *Well, so far you're not doing so well. Actually, you're batting zero. Every time you open your mouth you make things worse.*

But it didn't matter anymore. Pale Boy, who was now Abner, wasn't listening anymore. His mind was as gone as the old ways; his heart was as hard and black as a corroded carburetor.

The moonlight was brighter now. The clouds had sailed on. Pale Boy/Abner stepped down from his chair onto a rusted car roof and began to shape-shift rapidly. The popping of flesh and the creak of metal filled the night air and Batman felt the hair on his neck rise up and prick the interior of his cowl.

The moon passed in shadow again, and Pale Boy/Abner stood on his hind tires and stretched his tie rods and waved his fists—tires now—at the darkness, and the very air seemed full of the stench of hot oil and exhaust fumes. His head fell forward, his mouth full of and expanded with a bumper the color of a silver vein. And as the head fell, clanged on the roof of the car on which he stood, the Thunderbird stretched its front tires forward and they molded into little rubber claws, began to pull the car body forward. Pale Boy/Abner's eyes went wide and glassy and sprouted headlights.

The pyramid creaked and sighed beneath the Thunderbird's vast weight. A piece of a rusted automobile broke loose with a shriek and tumbled to the ground and rolled over and over. The top of the pyramid bowed toward the highway, shimmied, but held. Behind the dark windshield that was formed out of what had been Pale Boy/Abner's forehead (and as the moonlight struck it, a minor imperfection, a hairline crack, was visible), Batman saw shadowy movements, like frantic fish bodies slamming the sides of an inky bowl.

Batman slipped back into the Batmobile, fastened his seat belt, touched the engine to life, turned on the headlights.

The Thunderbird clamored down from the Pyramid and hit the ground at a run and with a roar. Musical notes jumped from the car like acrobats: Jan & Dean's "Dead Man's Curve."

There was no other choice but to ram the Thunderbird. Batman floorboarded the Batmobile. It leapt into the face of the Thunderbird. There was a noise like aluminum foil being wadded, another from the Thunderbird like a boxer taking a left to the solar plexus. The split in the windshield widened, was held together by a thin dark membrane. The Thunderbird rose up on its hind tires, exposed its underside, which had all the bumps and configurations of what belonged beneath a real car, and stagged back against the pyramid. The pyramid framework sagged and sighed and creaked and squeaked, but held.

The Thunderbird rebounded with a scream. It came forward throwing a left jab—a left tire—and the tire stretched waaaaaaaaaay out and popped the Batmobile's windshield and sprayed glass back in on Batman.

Batman ducked down and hit reverse and went back. The Batmobile tore a portion of the Thunderbird's bumper away as he did. The bumper fragments clattered to the ground, vibrated, were replaced by a fistful of bloody teeth lying in the dirt.

The Thunderbird, still on its hind tires, which were

spinning and driving it forward, bobbed and weaved and honked its horn, threw another left tire jab, followed it with a right tire cross that stretched the tie rods and the spindle and the tire itself.

The left glanced the Batmobile's roof. The right hit on the driver's side, splintering the window.

Batman stomped the brake, jerked the gearshift into first, stomped the accelerator, tried to ram again. There came a noise from under the Batmobile's hood like someone beating a seal to death with a club and the car clattered forward at a speed that would have embarrassed an amputee turtle. It hit the Thunderbird almost as hard as a bag of tossed marshmallows.

The Thunderbird motored a laugh as Jan & Dean finished out "Dead Man's Curve." It spread wide its front tires and grabbed the Batmobile by both doors and pushed, sealing Batman inside. The Batmobile's hood popped up like the hull of a cracked walnut. The Thunderbird let out a yell, slammed itself against the roof of the Batmobile.

Once.

Twice.

The Batmobile's roof dipped in.

The Thunderbird lifted the Batmobile, and with a twist of its flesh-metal body, slung it tumbling roof over tires into the car crusher, where it came to lie upright, its front end across the roof of a Plymouth already neatly tucked into the demolition saddle.

Batman spat blood on the dashboard. He coughed. Something seemed to be kicking his chest from the inside. Daggers were in his head and back. A tornado spun behind his wet left eye.

He glanced at the rearview mirror. Or where it was

supposed to be. It was gone. It was on the floorboard next to the accelerator. The front seat and Batman's lap were wearing the refuse of the front windshield and the roof was crushed far enough down in front it almost met the dashboard. Above him, it dipped almost to his head. Tight fit.

Part of the motor was visible through a wound in the hood. Radiator steam whistled whitely into the dark.

Batman turned his injured neck. It wasn't too hard to do that, no harder than carrying an elephant up the Washington Monument.

Through the cracked back glass, he saw the Thunderbird. It was on its hind tires, stalking forward like a confident sumo wrestler closing in for the kill.

Do something or lose it all, he thought. He reached for the EJECT button. If the roof release was ruined and it didn't throw the crumpled roof away, the eject seat would drive him into it so hard they would have to extricate his corpse from the car with a putty knife.

He continued to sit sideways in the seat, watching out the back window, waiting for the right moment. The Thunderbird's upper half was no longer visible, just its lower body. It was about to come down on the Batmobile, grab it and crush it.

Batman hit the EJECT button.

The blast caps tossed the roof high and hard, like a hat thrown in the excitement of a ball game. The seat launched after it, back and over the "head" of the upright Thunderbird. The seat was perfectly balanced so that it wouldn't flip. The rubber air cushion beneath it expanded with a hiss. The seat hit the ground hard, but the cushion took the bulk of the impact. Still, Batman felt his teeth clack together.

Unclamping his seat belt, he rolled from the chair, looked in the direction of the Batmobile. The Thunderbird's "back" was to him and it was still on its hind tires. It had its left front tire cocked and it punched down hard on the roof of the Batmobile. Then the right front tire struck the Batmobile, then the left, and the combinations continued. The Thunderbird was in a frenzy, beating the Batmobile's roof flat, smashing it down onto the car in the crusher's saddle. It either hadn't noticed his exit via ejection seat or didn't care and was taking it out on the car.

Batman tried to stand, wobbled, fell to one knee, put out a hand and touched . . . the remote.

He snatched it up. It looked okay. He had seen Pale Boy working it from atop the pyramid, making the crusher respond to his commands.

He glanced at the Thunderbird. The bully was leaning way over the Batmobile now, trouncing it with both tires.

Batman thumbed the ON button. The crusher whined. The saddle moved, sucked the Batmobile's front end into the machinery along with the Plymouth on which it was riding, as well as the left tire of the Thunderbird as it came down to strike another blow. There was a smashing sound, then the mewl of the Thunderbird's motor, followed by what was distinctly a human scream. Behind this came a mechanized screech, and the crusher jammed with a portion of the Batmobile hanging out of it.

The Thunderbird jerked back its left tire. Only it no longer had a tire. Black oil gushed from where the tire had connected to the chassis, spewed all over creation.

The Thunderbird spun around on its rear tires, the hood bending forward to bring the windshield low enough to spot its prey.

It saw Batman. Its hood opened and slammed shut rapidly and repeatedly, revealing an interior darker than its paint. Its underbelly heaved. Finally the hood hung open and a tongue the size of a foyer rug flicked out and licked what was left of its grillwork. Then the hood closed and the Thunderbird lowered its body to the ground, straightened itself, gunned forward on three wheels, the nub of its left tire punching up dust.

Batman was already moving. He darted for the pyramid. Went up it light and fast as a squirrel. The Thunderbird turned to pursue him, working at half speed, limping. Batman reached the wilting top of the pyramid, put a foot on the back of the chair, the seat of which, due to the shifting of the pyramid, was facing toward the edge of the deep drop.

Batman looked down. He saw the back of the billboard and the highway. A car went by in a flash of lights, a buzz of engine.

He looked back at the Thunderbird. It was climbing the pyramid, favoring its nub. Up it came, putting its front right tire out, forming a pincher, clenching metal with it, pushing with its hind tires. Slowly, steadily, oil dripping from its wound, it made its way up.

It paused, stretched its hood and windshield, trying to get a good look at its adversary.

Batman could see that the crack in the Thunderbird's windshield was wider yet. The membranes that had held it were ripped loose. A dark, featureless head was poking out of it, wriggling like a mole trying to work itself free from a too-tight hole. Shadows still slammed against the interior of the windshield, and something that looked like two black basketballs were rolling around behind the glass.

Eyes behind sunshades?

He could also hear the Thunderbird wheezing through its carburetor. The crusher had taken some wind out of it.

After a moment, it started up again. The pyramid rocked, shifted. Car pieces broke free and fell away.

The Thunderbird, nearly to the top, groped for Batman with its impossible tire, the rubber of it stretching to form a four-fingered hand. Batman stepped onto the back of the bent chair, just out of the way.

The Thunderbird pushed with its back tires to give it the added reach and—

As Batman expected, and counted on, the weight of the Thunderbird was too much. The pyramid leaned way back . . .

And fell apart.

Batman coiled his legs and leapt over the Thunderbird. He went wide of the falling pyramid, hit on his shoulder hard enough to feel it in the heels of his boots, then tumbled and came up on his feet.

He turned to see the Thunderbird tumbling over the edge of the drop. It scrambled with its hind tires, its one good front tire, but there was nothing to hold on to. The pyramid was no longer. It was a mass of separating junk and the junk went over the lip of the drop and splattered in all directions, and the Thunderbird went too, sailed a goodly distance through the air, hit the side of the great hill with the impact of a missile, bounced toward the billboard, struck the back of it and went through with a rip and a snap, and wearing Barrett's posterboard face over its hood, windshield, and roof, it hit the center stripe on the highway with an explosion of metal and oil. A lick of flame fluttered from its tail end, went out. The Thunderbird rolled and shed parts and ended up lying on its roof with the posterboard wrapped around its upper half, Barrett's spectacle-adorned face peering up at the night.

The Thunderbird lay there and trembled. Parts thrown out of it continued to roll and clank down the highway, then they quit clanking, made moist meaty noises, and eventually stopped traveling.

The Thunderbird weakly reached out with its one good tire and formed two huge fingers, pawed at the posterboard in the manner of a cat removing a cobweb. Barrett's image came loose, fluttered in the wind, went floating away into a roadside ditch.

The right front tire quivered, turned small and pallid, stretched wide on its spindle, flopped into the street palm up. Fingers twitched. Touched by the moonlight, it looked like an albino spider on its back, kicking its legs.

Now the Thunderbird was gone and there was only Pale Boy's naked body, ripped and battered, minus some internal organs. His left hand was smashed away and the nub of his wrist pumped dark oil, but only for an instant; the oil transformed to blood, continued to spew. His dimming eyes were on the sky.

The crack in his head was as wide as the edge of a fifty-cent piece and four inches long. From it fled one of the trapped souls he had pulled into it with his headlight eyes. Then another soul fled. And another. And another. All free and no longer part of the were-car's medicine.

Then Pale Boy felt his own soul letting loose. He

couldn't hold it. He lifted his head and opened his mouth and the dark form of it oozed over his broken and bloody bottom teeth, tugged itself out like a fat man rising from a recliner. Pale Boy tried to will it to return. The soul attempted to lower itself back inside, but before it could, an owl came out of the night and dove down swift as a bullet and clutched the soul in its talons and pulled it up and out and flew away with it.

No sooner had the owl vacated the scene than a video game and computer salesman from Gotham named Jack Headaway, driving his Volvo too fast and dodging car debris all over the road, zigged around a rusted Chevy and a pile of auto innards and clipped Pale Boy on the side of the head and knocked him up and under the Volvo and dragged him fifty yards before the body was thrown from beneath the car and into a roadside ditch—the same ditch where the fragment of the billboard bearing Barrett's face lay. Pale Boy lay on top of it and bled out the last of his blood.

Batman, down on one knee at the edge of the drop, had seen it all. He lifted his head and watched the owl pin itself before the moon, then dive out of the moonlight and into the all-embracing night.

The Owl God, he thought. *The real one*.

"I'm sorry, Pale Boy," he whispered. "I truly am."

He moved gingerly to a standing position. He had broken a rib in that jump and roll from the pyramid. It punched at his side like a drunk man making a point with the tip of his finger.

Batman removed the little flash from his belt, watched

the salesman get out of the Volvo with a flashlight of his own and run back to look into the ditch where Pale Boy had been thrown.

The salesman saw what was in the ditch, stiffened, walked back to the center of the highway, and threw up on the yellow line.

When the man finished cleansing his guts, Batman turned on his flash and blinked it at him. The salesman looked up, saw a shape like a giant bat standing on the high hill above, flashing a small flashlight.

Boy, thought the salesman, *is this one night or what?*

4

"I didn't see him. Really. I'd have stopped. I mean, I tried. There was all that junk—"

"I saw what happened," Batman said. "You're not to blame. Just hurry so we can get a crew back here to clean up that mess before someone wrecks."

The Volvo chugged over a hill, away from the rise that had held the Pyramid of Cars. As they went away, Batman had the urge to turn for a look, but his rib hurt too severely for that.

"You know," said the salesman, "you don't look so good, Mr. Batman."

"I'm not feeling particularly well, now that you mention it."

"Yeah, you need to see a doctor. . . . You know, I thought—and no offense now, okay?"

"Okay."

"I thought you'd be . . . well, bigger. Not that you're any dwarf. I just thought you'd be, like, bigger than life."

"No," Batman said. "No one's that big."

"I'm not sure what you mean."

But Batman didn't hear him. He had turned his head toward the passenger window and closed his eyes and isolated the pain and allowed himself to fall asleep.

Decelerate, Clutch, and—

—Downshift to the Epilogue

1

The Batcave, One Month Later

Bruce, finished recording last night's events in his journal, then sat back and eyed the packages on his desk. He had received them at police headquarters through Jim Gordon the night before, but until this morning he hadn't had time to examine either. One was a bundle. Most likely fan letters and hate mail. About once a month, Jim gathered up and packaged what came to the department for Batman, what didn't look explosive or dangerous, and gave it to him.

The other package was large, flat, and rectangular. Bruce tore it open. It was from Catherine Meadows. A note was inside. It read: *I thought you might want these. No one else has seen them. Catherine.*

It was the painting Angie had made of the Pyramid of Cars. It was broken in the middle, but Catherine had reinforced it from behind with a wooden slat and tape and had framed it. The tire tread mark that had marred the painting was gone. There was a smear of dried blood in its place. Pale Boy's blood.

Also inside the rectangular package was a little white book. On the front, written in black magic marker, was *The Book of the Thunderbird*. Inside were the entries Pale Boy had written as Abner.

Bruce spot-read some of it, and even now, a month later, he felt a surge of depression. He knew why Catherine hadn't shown it to the Gotham Police or anyone else. There was no need to sully Pale Boy's reputation further. And who was going to believe Pale Boy had become a Ford Thunderbird, except possibly Jim Gordon? It was best to let people think Pale Boy had lost his mind and murdered with a car, not transformed into one.

The case was closed; the crazed hit-and-run killer was gone for good.

Bruce put the book down, picked up the painting again.

One for the trophy case. It and the journal, perhaps. To go along with the reminders of his most unique adventures. And this had certainly been a unique one.

He put the painting down and thought, *Poor Pale Boy. Devoured by darkness. As we are all devoured by it in time*. It all seemed so pointless. The day-to-day struggle. Eventually it ends the same for everyone. The good, the bad, the ugly. Everyone gets the same reward.

Darkness.

He looked at the bundle Gordon had given him with Catherine's package. He was right about its contents. Mail.

He shuffled the letters, but felt no real desire to open them. He wasn't up to being told how great he was, or how rotten he was.

Then he saw that one letter had a postmark from Nebraska, no return address on the envelope.

Mandy?

He opened it.

Yes, Mandy.

It read:

Dear Batman:

I'm sending this to you through the Gotham Police Department. I hope it reaches you.

I wanted you to know that just when I thought my life was worthless and there was nothing to live for, nothing for my child to live for, when I thought a needle in my veins was the answer, when no one wanted to help and there was no institution to turn to, you came along.

It hasn't been easy here back in Nebraska, but it's certainly been better than the streets of Gotham City. My parents haven't changed. I pass them on the street and they look away. It's as if I'm dead. I don't believe they will ever change, and I'm trying to learn to live with that.

I have a part-time secretarial job at a feed and seed store—no kidding!—and I'm going to college part time, and Kerrie is in day care the three times a week I work. Soon I hope we'll move out of the little duplex where we live and rent an apartment or a house. Kerrie is growing so fast, and I would like for her to have her own room when she's older.

Life isn't perfect, but I have friends and am-

> bitions, and now the world looks much brighter than it did before. It looks worth the living.
>
> I owe that to you. For a moment there, everything looked like a lie. I almost lost hope. You gave it back to me. You gave me my second chance. I sincerely hope this reaches you. I send all my love and gratitude.
>
> From the bottom of my heart,
>
> Mandy

Bruce folded the letter carefully and returned it to the envelope.

He thought, *And then again, maybe it doesn't matter where we all end up. What counts is how we get there and what we do to make the trip better for ourselves and others.*

He realized suddenly that he felt good. Not since the night he had put Mandy and her baby on the bus back to Nebraska had he felt such a surge of hope. Mandy's letter had given him that rare, old-time rush, when it felt as if it all mattered and he made a difference, that the world wasn't entirely random and mad.

He would include the letter in a glass case with the painting and *The Book of the Thunderbird*. Somehow he felt the contrasting feelings they gave him belonged together.

Yin and yang.

He reached for the console next to the computer, flicked a switch, plunged the cave into a darkness so complete he couldn't see his hand in front of his face—a darkness akin to nothingness.

He leaned back in his chair, thought, *What's so bad*

about darkness? It's my element. From darkness we come, to darkness we return. A round-trip ticket.

Closing his eyes, he let the cool calm of the dark embrace him. He felt as if he were waiting somewhere inside someone's dream—his own, perhaps—waiting patiently for that dreaming someone, or himself, to create the Batman and make something happen.

Ladies and Gentlemen, Cut Your Engines